MONSTER SWAP

Robbie and Voxy
Zainab and Mash
Eddie and Fenda

Eddie and Fenda

Written by
JONNY ZUCKER

Illustrated by
TONY ROSS

*Hodder
Children's
Books*

A division of Hachette Children's Books

To the Nottingham Posse: Ellis Guilford Secondary, Ambleside
Primary, Heathfield Primary, Old Basford Primary, Whitemoor
Primary, Hempshill Primary, Rosslyn Park Primary

Text copyright © 2012 Jonny Zucker
Illustrations copyright © 2012 Tony Ross

First published in Great Britain in 2012
by Hodder Children's Books

ISBN: 978 0 340 99712 3

Book design by Janette Revill
Printed and bound by CPI Group (UK) Ltd, Croydon, CR0 4YY

Hodder Children's Books
A division of Hachette Children's Books
338 Euston Road, London NW1 3BH
An Hachette UK company
www.hachette.co.uk

CONTENTS

Eddie and the
Bone-Jangling
Funfair **3**

Fenda and the Fiery
Catering Fiasco **103**

After thousands of years spent hidden from human eyes, the earth's monsters have finally revealed themselves. From the murkiest swamps to the deepest forests, the monsters have emerged.

At first, humans were frightened of monsters. After all, seeing a giant purple two-headed monster dribbling mucus through your kitchen window would be enough to put any human off their cornflakes.

And at first, monsters were frightened of humans too. After all, seeing a tiny red-faced toddler human screaming for ice cream would be enough to put any monster off their sour cabbage and soil burgers.

So monsters set up the **MONSTER COUNCIL FOR UNDERSTANDING HUMANS** and humans set up the **Human Agency for Understanding Monsters**. Both organizations agreed that if monsters and humans were to stop being scared of each other they needed to find out as much as they could about each other's lives.

So they arranged a series of exchange visits. These 'Swaps' would involve a human child visiting a monster child in their monster world, followed by that same monster child visiting the human child in *their* world. No one had any idea how these visits would turn out ...

Welcome to the world of

EDDIE
and the
BONE-
JANGLING
FUNFAIR

Dear Fenda and family

Thank you so much for agreeing to host the visit of Eddie Wright, Fenda's human exchange partner. Eddie is very much looking forward to his visit, but I must warn you not to be taken aback by certain of his human behaviours and skills. For a start he is a mad puzzle fiend, so if he starts taking your home apart and piecing it back together, he will be doing this with the very best of intentions. He is an expert at kung-fu (a human martial art) so if he challenges any  of you to a fight it is NOT because he doesn't like you. In addition he possesses just the one tongue so I'd be grateful if you wouldn't throw him hundreds of feet into the air when he uses this for both sweet and savoury foods.

I gather that Eddie's visit coincides with Pembran Festival Day, which I know is an occasion to overeat and generally act wildly. Please could you ensure he doesn't eat too many Grub-Mash Smoothies during the festivities as his family would like him to return to the human world the same size and shape he was before he arrived in your settlement.

Wishing you a splendid time during Eddie's visit.

Yours sincerely

Lady Bug Gazap

MONSTER COUNCIL FOR UNDERSTANDING HUMANS

1

Eddie took a swig from his water bottle. It had been a long walk from the train station and he'd now reached the meeting-point marked on the map.

But there were no monsters in sight.

All he could see was a huge expanse of peach-coloured sand with several large holes spread across its surface.

As a mad puzzle fiend, Eddie never travelled without one. He pulled a complex metal puzzle out of his pocket and tried to unlock the three inter-connected sections. He was on the verge of cracking it when he heard a faint rumbling sound in the distance. This got louder and louder until it reached a raucous crescendo. A second later, what looked like a giant blue pig with spikes on its back shot out of one of the holes. It landed with a crash on the sand and threw off the green monster it was carrying on its back. The monster threw the pig-thing six small white balls then the pig-thing turned, ran a few paces and disappeared into one of the other holes.

'HEY EDDIE, I'M FENDA!' shouted the monster, sweeping sand off her fur before springing over to him with a magnificently high leap, and throwing her two thick arms around his midriff for a bone-crushing hug.

Eddie felt the air being sucked out of him as he gaped in awe at his monster-swap partner.

Fenda was three feet tall and five feet wide. Her three eyes were arranged in a triangle formation on her head. Her three feet were incredibly flat with tiny springs on the underside

and her arms ended in flattened paws with ten wrinkly fingers.

'H … H … Hi Fenda,' said Eddie, barely able to breathe.

'Brilliant to meet you!' grinned Fenda, finally letting go of him.

Eddie took a deep lungful of air, dropped the metal puzzle back into his pocket, and looked over Fenda's shoulder to the spot where the pig-thing had disappeared.

Fenda followed his gaze. 'That was a Porcupig,' she explained. 'They live in lots of monster clans. We Pembran monsters use them as a taxi service to take us from our settlement up to the surface.'

'What were those little white things you gave him?' asked Eddie.

'They're ear wax balls,' explained Fenda. 'We call them Waxies. They're what we use for money round here. Each of our ears produces two Waxies a day. You can either spend them or save them!'

'Er … are we going straight down to your settlement then?' asked Eddie.

'Absolutely,' nodded Fenda.

'So why didn't that Porcupig wait around to take us there?'

'Because on the way down,' grinned Fenda, 'we don't need Porcupigs!'

She grabbed Eddie's elbow and raced across the sand to the hole where the Porcupig had vanished, and dived in headfirst.

'WAAAAAAAAAAAAA!' screamed Eddie as he toppled in after her and found himself hurtling downwards at phenomenal speed inside a circular chute with very smooth curved walls.

'ULTRA FINE!' shrieked Fenda with delight, holding Eddie's elbow very tightly as they twisted and spun.

Thirty seconds later they shot out of the hole and skidded to a halt on a large bed of soft grey mud.

'Welcome to the Pembran monster clan!' beamed Fenda, yanking Eddie to his feet. 'This is the Travel Circle.'

They were standing in a gigantic, circular underground cavern, dotted with chutes marked '**UPWARDS**' and '**DOWNWARDS**'. The place was illuminated by shafts of light coming from holes up above that weren't connected to any chutes. The ground was covered in orange moss which felt warm to the feet. The Porcupig who'd taken Fenda to the surface was comparing his day's Waxie takings with a couple of his mates. Several other Porcupigs were sipping bone shakes or sitting in huddles by the bottom of different tunnels.

'I got the last Porcupig of the day,' said Fenda with satisfaction.

Nearby Eddie could hear voices and the thud of feet. 'Where's all that noise coming from?' he asked.

'That's the Market Square,' explained Fenda,

beginning to walk in the opposite direction. 'It's late night opening today but we'll go there another time.'

'Cool,' nodded Eddie, following his monster tour guide.

'You've come at a very important time,' said Fenda, leaving the Circle and guiding Eddie down a narrow rocky passage. 'It's the annual Pembran Festival in a few days.'

'What do you *do* on Festival Day?' asked Eddie, looking above him at the strange purple plants growing down from the roof of the passage and spitting out hot, acidic drips which Fenda skipped to avoid. Eddie thought it would be wise to do the same.

'We eat loads, play loads and feel ill for about two weeks after!' laughed Fenda.

A short while later Eddie spied a sleek grey creature in the passage up ahead, with glowing amber eyes and very sharp teeth that glistened in its bendy snout. It looked like a mongoose gone to the dark side.

'GET OUTTA HERE!' shouted Fenda loudly. The grey shape twisted round and in a flash was gone from sight.

'What was that?' asked Eddie nervously.

'It's a Grim Grim Coyote,' explained Fenda. 'Only a few ever dare to come anywhere near our settlement. If you visit the Open Plains though, there are loads of them. They hunt in packs and guess what their favourite food is?'

'No idea,' replied Eddie.

'Pembran monsters!' said Fenda.

Eddie shivered and moved a bit closer to Fenda. 'So where are we going?' he asked.

'There's someone I want you to meet,' said Fenda.

The narrow passage ended and they stepped out on to the bottom of a large grey hill which was studded with enormous flashing light-blue mushrooms.

'Don't eat any of those,' warned Fenda, 'they rip your insides out and your outsides in!'

Eddie swerved round a particularly large mushroom and followed Fenda. They raced upwards and at the hill's summit found themselves looking down on to a huge pink valley, with a very deep expanse of the orangey moss on its floor.

Bang in the middle of the valley was a gigantic monster fairground, the centrepiece of which was a huge rollercoaster made entirely from different-sized bones. It had a giant sign at the top, each letter of which was made from different coloured fragments of wood:

THE MONSTER WORLD'S FINEST
ZOOM-A-COASTER!
CAN YOU MAKE IT ROUND IN ONE PIECE?

Surrounding this were lots of other attractions – a shooting range with short red guns made out of animal horns, a bumper car ride with seaweed cars on *the ceiling* and a slot machine arcade where you put your *head* into a socket and the machines spun *you* round.

But although Eddie was bowled over by all of the rides and machines, he could see that the place had enjoyed far better days. In fact, as he and Fenda walked down the hill towards the fair, he spotted loose joints, broken wheels and crumbling pillars. Close up, it looked as if the entire enterprise could fall apart at any minute. They proceeded down the funfair's main walkway and stopped at the base of the Zoom-a-Coaster, where a wizened old Pembran stood with his back to them, wailing at the top of his voice.

'IT'S ALL OVER!' groaned the aged monster with pain and anguish, 'WE'RE DOOMED, FINISHED, KAPUT!'

'D**ON'T BE SAD, GRANDPA ZEBU!**' shouted Fenda, throwing her arms around the old Pembran's neck, 'IT'S *SO* NOT OVER – AT LEAST NOT YET!'

The old Pembran's top eye spun round to the back of his head and came to rest on Fenda and her human pal.

'Fenda!' he cried, swivelling back his top eye to rejoin the others and turning his body round to face the new arrivals. 'And this must be Elvis!'

'Er … it's actually Eddie,' said Eddie, shaking

Grandpa Zebu's paw. 'Why were you saying it's all over?'

Grandpa Zebu sighed and indicated for all three of them to sit on the ground. The orange moss felt toasty but not too hot.

'This funfair has been in our family for over a hundred years,' explained Grandpa Zebu, 'but times have been tough and as you can see it's fallen into disrepair. We simply haven't made enough money in the last few years to update and repair it.'

'But surely you can get the money some way?' said Eddie.

'We've tried very hard,' replied Fenda. 'My mum and dad are visiting other monster clans at this very minute trying to raise funds, but so far they've had zero luck.'

'With Festival Day nearly upon us and no cash in sight, it looks like we've reached the end of the path,' said Grandpa sadly. 'It breaks my heart but what can we do?'

'In the human world we sometimes use local celebrities to be the face of campaigns to save things like parks and libraries,' said Eddie. 'Isn't there a Pembran celebrity who could do that for you?'

'There is someone,' said Fenda, 'but he and Grandpa fell out years ago.'

'Kubby Jonks is his name,' said Grandpa wistfully. 'He's one of the most famous artists in the entire monster world. He paints with his nostrils and his work goes for thousands of Waxies.'

'Why did you fall out?' asked Eddie.

'Many, many years ago, when I first took over the fair from *my* father, Kubby lodged with me for three months,' explained Grandpa. 'I wanted to make the fair more modern so things were being built and taken apart all over the place. I was pretty poor at the time and Kubby had promised to pay me rent. But one day he just upped and left without any payment at all. I was stunned – I'd thought we were friends. I was so furious that although he tried to talk to me soon after, I wouldn't have it.'

'And you haven't spoken to him since, have you?' cut in Fenda.

Grandpa Zebu shook his head sadly.

They sat in silence for a few moments, then Grandpa stood up. 'Look, Fenda, let's forget about the funfair for a minute – we have a HUMAN guest here. We need to go and get this young man something to eat and give him a proper Pembran welcome!'

'You're right,' nodded Fenda.

Up the hill and down the other side they walked, back along the narrow passage and out into the Travel Circle which was now completely empty. It was getting dark up above on the surface so the light coming from the ceiling holes was fading quickly.

On the far side of the Circle was a small gate carved into a wall. They walked through this and stepped on to a wide bridge which passed over some fast-flowing silver water below. Eddie spotted several gigantic white fish with remarkably thin bodies, twisting from side to side as they battled the fierce current.

After crossing the bridge they went through a second gate and emerged into a huge area – this one filled with lots of large spheres. The spheres themselves were made from small stones welded together and covered in stubbly maroon plants – the kind you might come across in deep sea diving excursions. Some of the spheres were vast, some were of medium size and some were pretty tiny.

They stopped in front of a medium-sized one.

'Welcome to Grandpa's abode!' smiled Fenda, pulling open a small door. 'We're staying with him because my mum and dad are away.'

Eddie stepped inside. It took his eyes a few seconds to adjust to the darkness. Grandpa

reached up, touched something and a strong
bluish light came on. Eddie spotted a blue slug
sitting on a wooden bar on the ceiling of the
sphere whose mouth Grandpa had just pulled
open. It was from this mouth that the light was
shining.

'I'll just get some supper,' said Fenda, going
outside, plucking several plants off the walls
and coming back in. She handed two each to
Grandpa and Eddie and kept two for herself.
They all sat down on the floor of the sphere

and Fenda and Grandpa started chewing on the plants with relish.

'You're eating the walls of your house?' asked Eddie in surprise.

'Don't worry,' said Fenda with her mouth full, 'they'll grow back before you can say ecologically-sound-living-habitat.'

Eddie took a deep breath and nibbled a corner of one of his plants. To his delight it was absolutely delicious – like a mix between a pancake and a pizza.

'Amazing!' he murmured.

'We use our savoury tongues to eat these,' slurped Fenda, 'and our sweet tongues to eat the treats and desserts we make for each other's birthdays and on special occasions.'

'Two tongues are better than one!' grinned Eddie, who could have done with an extra tongue so that he could eat two meals at the same time.

'Here, have more!' said Fenda, nipping outside, ripping another plant from the wall and stuffing it into his hand.

In the end Eddie had four of the maroon plants, Grandpa Zebu had three and Fenda had five. After they'd finished chewing they sat with their backs against the wall of the sphere, feeling full and contented.

'We'd better get some sleep,' said Grandpa, climbing up the side of the sphere and curling his feet around two wooden bars affixed to the wall. His body draped down and he swung for a few seconds until he fell still, like a giant green bat.

Fenda climbed the opposite wall, and attached her feet to another two bars. 'There's a perch for you,' she yawned, pointing to a third set of wooden bars.

'Er … is it OK if I sleep on the floor?' said Eddie.

'Of course!' nodded Fenda.

Grandpa let out a loud snore.

The floor wasn't quite as comfy as Eddie's

bed back home but it would definitely do. He
went outside and pulled another few plants off
the wall, chuckling to himself as another set
grew back in their places. He went back in,
folded the plants into a pillow shape, stretched
out until he got comfy, and closed his eyes.

Eddie was woken the next morning by a loud rapping on the sphere's front door. Grandpa Zebu and Fenda were still fast asleep. The knocking sounded again a few seconds later, only this time it was much louder. When the door was still not opened, whoever it was outside gave it the most thunking great kick and the sphere was sent violently spinning. Grandpa and Fenda fell off their sleep perches and Eddie did four forward rolls in rapid succession.

Finally the sphere smacked into a wall and crashed to a halt.

A furious Fenda leapt to her feet and yanked open the door. Standing outside were three Pembran monsters. Each of them had extra-long hair on top of their heads that had been gelled to a point. They wore shiny black ten-fingered gloves on their paws and sneering expressions on their faces.

'HOW DARE YOU KICK OUR HOME, YOU HORRIBLE BRUTES!' yelled Fenda,

looking at them with disgust. 'AND ANYWAY, WE'RE NOT IN, SO CLEAR OFF!'

'We're not here to see you, Waxie Face, we're here to see your grandfather,' said the biggest one, wedging his foot in the door and speaking in a voice so oily it sounded like it had been fried several times that morning.

Grandpa Zebu nudged Fenda to one side and stood at the door, with Eddie peeping over his shoulder. Eddie flexed his muscles. He was a kung-fu expert and figured that his chops and kicks might be needed at any moment to deal with these unpleasant monsters.

'The Vultrain Brothers!' sighed Grandpa. 'Vix, Vep and Vad … I might have guessed!'

'We've come here to offer you a job, old monster,' said Vix – the largest one – with a patronizing smile on his lips.

'What are you talking about?' demanded Fenda angrily.

'Since your funfair is falling apart,' said Vep

– the middle one – 'we've been secretly building our own one in Falli-Fatti Canyon and it's very nearly finished! There's a bit more building work but it will definitely be ready by Festival Day!'

'THAT IS SO NOT ULTRA FINE!' snarled Fenda with a mixture of shock and anger. 'THERE CAN'T BE ANOTHER FUNFAIR IN THE PEMBRAN SETTLEMENT!'

'I agree,' said Vix, 'one is enough and from now on, that one will be ours! We're just being really, really generous in offering the old boy a job cleaning the seats of our brand-new Zoom-a-Coaster for one Waxie per day. Is that super-kind or what?'

'But that was the job you did at Grandpa's funfair before he sacked you for stealing Grub-Mash Smoothies!' protested Fenda. 'And anyway he paid you *seven* Waxies a day!'

'The theft was never proved,' said Vix curtly.

'The economic climate is harsher now,' said Vep.

'Whatever the other two said,' added Vad.

'A … a … new funfair?' stuttered Grandpa.

'That's right, old bean,' smiled Vix. 'Somewhere a Pembran would be proud to be seen, not like your old rubbish dump!'

'This conversation is over!' shouted Fenda.

'I think not,' said Vix, but Fenda slammed the sphere door shut in their faces, shaking with rage.

'If you change your mind, you know where to find us!' called out Vix before he and his brothers sauntered away, laughing among themselves.

'The total creeps!' hissed Fenda. 'I'd like to put THEM in a Grub-Mash Smoothie!'

'We'd better take a look at their funfair,' said Grandpa anxiously.

'Relax,' said Fenda. 'There was nothing in Falli-Fatti Canyon when I was last there, and that was only a couple of months ago. They won't have had time to build anything decent.'

But half an hour later when they reached

Falli-Fatti Canyon – a huge U-shaped scoop to the east of the main Pembran settlement – they were completely spellbound by the Vultrain brothers' new attraction. Although it needed some finishing touches it was already spectacular. Their Zoom-a-Coaster was twice as big as Grandpa's. There was a massive Fling-Wheel that could shoot a monster two hundred feet into the air. A huge Teeth-Floss stall sat next to a Skin-Bashing Tunnel that looked far more scary and impressive than anything in Grandpa's fair.

'It's not *that* good,' tutted Fenda.

'We're doomed!' muttered Grandpa miserably.

'Don't worry,' said Fenda defiantly. 'We'll raise the money to fix your place and make it a million times better than their rubbish set-up.'

'There's not much time though, is there?' murmured Eddie.

'I'm going back to my fair to sit forlornly and mull over lost opportunities,' sighed Grandpa sadly.

He trudged off one way, while Fenda pulled Eddie in the opposite direction.

A few minutes later they arrived in the Market Square and Eddie stood completely still for a few seconds, transfixed by the mad hustle and bustle in front of him. Stalls were set out on all four sides of the square. One had a Pembran monster giving another monster a massage on his back with two giant hammers, one was a hairdresser's where two monsters were brushing knots out of a third's very knotty under-foot hair, one was selling different-sized monster hats made from some sort of golden, wafer-thin fabric, another had a monster in a white coat checking another monster's teeth with an implement as big as a small tractor. Waxies were changing paws at a very rapid rate.

'This way,' said Fenda as she and Eddie

weaved between buyers and sellers. They hurried round the back of a stall selling hot lava sandwiches and followed a snaking path until they came to a row of small tin huts that were nowhere near as bright and welcoming as the stalls in the square.

'This is a bit desperate, but we don't have much choice,' whispered Fenda, stopping in front of a particularly shabby-looking hut and knocking on the door.

They heard a grunt and the door was pulled open a fraction. The face of a huge Pembran chewing a long piece of green corn appeared in the crack.

'What do you want?' asked the face suspiciously.

'It's me, Fenda – Grandpa Zebu's grand-daughter. We've come to talk money, Sproggy.'

A couple of chains were undone and the door opened fully. Sproggy ushered Fenda and Eddie in and shut the door behind them. It was dim inside and the only objects were a small table and a safe on the wall.

'Erm … I've heard that you lend money to monsters for outrageous rates of interest,' said Fenda, 'and I need to borrow some very urgently.'

'What do you want it for?' enquired Sproggy. 'Is it for kid's stuff – Cheese Lollies, Bored Games – that sort of thing?'

'Not quite,' replied Fenda, 'it's more for things like repairing an old Zoom-a-Coaster and updating a rotating Pembran-swinging slot machine.'

Sproggy wiped his nose with a paw and walked over to the safe. 'I *would* have been able to help you a couple of weeks ago, but my stock is very low.'

He flicked open the safe door.

There were about twelve Waxies in there.

Fenda's mouth dropped open.

'The Vultrain brothers pretty much cleared me out,' explained Sproggy with a shrug of his shoulders.

Fenda looked as if someone had just poured a wet weekend over her head.

'Try Elfrith a couple of doors down,' said Sproggy. 'He might have a stash of Waxies.'

But it was the same at Elfrith's and at all of the other Pembran loan sharks in the row. The Vultrains had got to all of them first and had almost completely snaffled up their funds. By mid afternoon, Eddie and Fenda were in a pit of despair. Fenda ran back to Grandpa's sphere to get some of her mud sculptures to sell to stall holders, but the only offers she got for them were a packet of stale orange moss crisps and the opportunity to take a bath with a large family of extra-filthy Porcupigs.

It was nightfall by the time they returned home, tired and defeated.

Grandpa Zebu was waiting for them in the sphere and their hearts sank when they saw his expectant face.

'Anything?' he asked, with a wisp of hope in his voice.

They shook their heads.

'Oh dear,' he said quietly.

'Maybe we'll think of something tomorrow,' said Eddie optimistically.

'Or maybe not,' said Fenda, walking outside, pulling some plants off the sphere walls and chucking one down her throat before climbing up to her bed perch.

Eddie didn't really feel that hungry either, so he also ate just one plant and settled down to sleep. As he twisted to get comfortable his heart was full of despair at the thought of the smarmy Vultrains doing a roaring trade on Festival Day while Grandpa's funfair would be standing barren and empty.

Eddie woke early the next morning and as Fenda and Grandpa Zebu were still asleep, he started making a Rubik's Cube type puzzle with sections of several plants he pulled off the sphere walls. He was well on the way to finishing it when a genius money-making idea exploded in his head.

'I'VE GOT IT!' he cried, pulling Fenda off her perch.

'Got what?' asked Fenda sleepily.

'Come on!' urged Eddie. 'There's no time to waste!'

He raced to the Travel Circle with a very tired Fenda close behind. When they arrived they found a large number of Porcupigs sleeping near the bases of the upward tunnels.

'So why are we here?' demanded Fenda.

Eddie strode straight up to an elderly Pembran couple who had just arrived and were about to wake a Porcupig to ask for a ride to the surface.

'Good morning!' smiled Eddie, running over to them. 'How would you like to travel to the surface for just *four* Waxies today?'

'That would be very useful, as we're saving up to buy toenail clippers that double as a radio,' replied the female Pembran.

'Yes,' nodded the male. 'Which Porcupig do we take for this lower rate?'

'You won't be taking a Porcupig today, Madam,' smiled Eddie, 'you'll be taking a HUMAN!'

Fenda gaped at Eddie as he got on to all

fours and positioned himself at the bottom of one of the upward tunnels.

The elderly Pembrans climbed gingerly on to Eddie's back.

'Could you shrink yourselves and make it a bit easier for this special human transportation vehicle?' asked Fenda, nodding with admiration at Eddie's money-making scheme.

'Certainly,' nodded the female. Eddie watched in astonishment as the elderly couple squeezed their noses and in an instant shrank to about a tenth of their usual size.

'Incredible!' whispered Eddie. 'Can you do that too, Fenda?'

'Of course!' she replied. 'But not now because I think you should get going.'

'Cool,' replied Eddie. 'See you in a bit.'

He waved goodbye and crawled into the mouth of the tunnel with the elderly Pembrans on his back.

'Go for it!' called Fenda.

The surface of the upward chutes was far less smooth than the downward ones and Eddie found he could get a decent grip. Five minutes later he emerged at the top and gently lowered his passengers down.

'What a lovely ride!' smiled the female as she and her fellow traveller slapped themselves on their foreheads and returned to their normal size. The female handed Eddie four Waxies. He dropped them into his jacket pocket before locating the nearest downward hole and leaping headfirst into it. Fenda was waiting for him at the bottom. He handed her the Waxies. 'I know it's not much,' he said, 'but it's a start.'

By now the Porcupigs were stirring, but Eddie got in first when teenage twin Pembran sisters appeared. Eddie did his sales pitch and the girls willingly accepted his reduced-cost offer.

But as Eddie got down and the Pembrans climbed on to his back, an angry-looking

Porcupig marched over. 'Hey, those are our customers!' he protested.

'There's no law that says you HAVE to travel to the surface by Porcupig,' hit back Fenda, 'so there's NOTHING you can do about it!'

'Well, I don't like it and my fellow Porcupigs won't like it one little bit!' snapped the Porcupig.

This second journey went smoothly for Eddie and he pocketed four more Waxies. But by the time he got down Fenda was completely surrounded by irate Porcupigs all snapping in gruff voices about the unwanted new human taxi.

'Don't get your prickles in a twist,' snapped Fenda, 'a bit of competition is no bad thing for you lot!'

The Porcupigs looked at her with outrage.

'All right, all right, we'll go,' she conceded, unravelling her arms to five times their usual length and pushing the Porcupigs back, an act that stunned Eddie.

The Porcupigs grunted and moaned but backed off while Fenda and Eddie stepped over to a tunnel that had no Pembrans or Porcupigs at its base.

'Love the arms thing,' grinned Eddie, as Fenda withdrew them, 'and here's four more Waxies.'

'The human lift project was a great idea,' said Fenda gratefully, 'but I don't want to provoke a Pembran v Porcupig war.'

They started walking and after turning a corner came upon a large, crooked building on their right, with a wonky sign stating **THE BONE AND BEAST**. Weird warbling music was drifting out of its windows.

'What's that?' asked Eddie.

'It's a drinking house,' replied Fenda, 'best to avoid it.'

'What's the music?'

'They have live bands on and ...'

'I LOVE live music!' exclaimed Eddie, hurrying towards the door.

'No … wait!' shouted Fenda, but he was already inside and she had no option other than to follow him in.

The smell was the first thing that hit Eddie. It was a mixture of sour milk, fried onions and soggy newspapers. Sitting at tables were lots of Pembran monsters drinking from very long thin glasses filled with some sort of yellow sludge. Behind the bar stood a huge and menacing Pembran with an earring through one of his paws. He was alternating between pouring drinks and hitting misbehaving monsters on the head with a large silver tray.

On a small stage at the far side of the room was a sign stating:

IF YOU LAST LONGER THAN A MINUTE ON THE STAGE, YOU WILL WIN A BIG CASH PRIZE!

At that moment a nervous-looking young female Pembran was sitting down on the stage holding a small two-stringed rope guitar.

'This one is called Slug Cheese Festival,' she said, in a voice not much louder than a whisper. She plucked one of the guitar strings and started singing in a high-pitched, croaky voice.

A huge male Pembran with a heavy silver neck chain was standing at the side of the stage. He listened to her warbling for a few seconds then grabbed her by the ear and threw her over his shoulder. She crashed over the bar, just missing the landlord, and landed with her head in a bucket of ice.

'WHO'S NEXT?' bellowed the silver chain monster.

'WE ARE!' called Eddie, racing towards the stage, climbing on to it and grabbing the rope guitar. Fenda shook her head violently but when Eddie didn't move, reluctantly she joined him up there.

'*What are you doing?*' she hissed.

'Just improvise,' replied Eddie, who was a fairly decent guitar player in the human world and had ambitions of becoming a pop star at the very least or, failing that, a judge on a musical TV talent show. The rope guitar was tuned very strangely though and the only notes he managed to get out of it were grating and screechy.

As soon as he started playing, Fenda began throwing herself around the stage, performing crazy dance moves, back flips, handstands and pirouettes.

They'd only been on for about fifteen seconds when the neck-chain Pembran grabbed them by their necks and threw them over his shoulder. They flew through the air and straight out of the nearest window, landing on a large bale of straw in the Bone and Beast's courtyard.

'Oh well,' said Eddie, 'at least we tried.'

With just eight Waxies to their name, they walked back towards the Travel Circle, where Porcupig business was now brisk. They were only halfway across the Circle when there was suddenly a gigantic explosion of noise. A split second later a vast collection of wood and metal came crashing out of the mouth of one of the downward chutes and went hurtling straight towards Eddie and Fenda's heads.

5

Eddie used a powerful and super fast kung-fu chop to smash a huge length of wood out of their way, grabbed Fenda and leaped sideways, avoiding the rest of the cascading objects by a fraction of a millimetre.

'WHAT IN PEMBRANS' NAME IS GOING ON?' demanded Fenda furiously as the chunks of wood and metal lunged to a stop.

'Step out of the way, peasants!' ordered three oily voices. 'Special delivery for us!'

'Surprise, surprise!' snarled Fenda as the Vultrain boys marched into view, each pushing a large stone trolley.

'You could have killed us, if it wasn't for Eddie's amazing kung-fu and leaping sideways skills!' thundered Fenda.

'Where was the warning?' demanded Eddie.

'Warnings are for wimps,' replied Vix curtly.

'And while you two have time to stand around and do nothing, we have a gleaming new funfair to finish,' laughed Vep.

'Whatever the other two said,' added Vad.

Eddie and Fenda watched helplessly as the Vultrain brothers loaded all of the fresh building materials on to their stone trolleys and started lugging it away in the direction of Falli-Fatti Canyon.

'This is maddening!' snapped Fenda, shaking her fists at them. 'Festival Day is going to be completely ruined. My parents won't be here, Grandpa will be totally down in the dumps and the Vultrains will be busy becoming Waxie millionaires.'

'Speaking of your parents,' said a Porcupig, ambling over with a piece of bark resting on his back.

'What have you got there?' asked Fenda.

'A Post-Jackal gave this to me to deliver to you,' replied the Porcupig, shaking the bark off his back.

Fenda picked it up and she and Eddie studied the spidery writing carved into the bark's surface.

Dear Fenda,

Have had absolutely no luck anywhere – even got chased out of the Erubi monster settlement because they thought we were selling mucus insurance. Really hope you and Grandpa are having better luck and that Eddie arrived safely. Send him our warmest wishes and tell him we're looking forward to meeting him. Sorry not to bring better news.

Love M&D

Half an hour later Eddie and Fenda were sitting outside Grandpa Zebu's sphere rolling a stone backwards and forwards to each other, discussing last-gasp ideas to try and raise funds.

'We could suck the Waxies out of other Pembrans' ears with long straws,' suggested Fenda.

'They'd just beat us up,' replied Eddie.

'Oh yeah,' nodded Fenda.

'How about making Waxies out of some other material?' suggested Fenda.

'Nothing can replicate ear wax,' sighed Eddie.

They sat there glumly, swapping madcap and totally impractical ideas, while they waited for Grandpa to get home. Half an hour later he hadn't shown. An hour later there was still no sign of him.

'Let's go down to the fair and get him,' said Fenda a trifle anxiously when it started getting dark.

They hardly spoke as they made their way down the passage and up the hill. When they reached the fair they looked for Grandpa but he wasn't around.

'He must be here somewhere,' said Eddie.

Together they searched the rides and arcades but drew a blank.

'I don't like this,' shivered Fenda, 'he's never gone missing before.'

'We'll find him,' said Eddie.

But Fenda wasn't listening.

'Grandpa!' she yelled at the very top of her voice. **'GRANDPA!!!'**

They raced back to Grandpa Zebu's sphere but he still wasn't there.

'Where is he?' asked Fenda, beginning to panic. 'What if something bad has happened to him?'

'Are you looking for the old fellow?' shouted a father Pembran washing lice into his son's hair.

Fenda nodded.

'I saw him earlier at the Bone and Beast,' replied the dad. 'He looked a bit the worse for wear.'

'Let's go!' urged Fenda, breaking into a run.

Luckily they didn't have to go inside the Bone and Beast again because Grandpa Zebu was sitting on a large rock outside, drinking from two tall glasses simultaneously and singing an old Pembran folk song at the top of his voice.

SHE was a lovely Pembran girl
Had a Porcupig called Swirl
But she lied and lied and lied
And the Porcupig just died

'Grandpa!' scolded Fenda, taking the glasses out of his hand and emptying the yellow sludge on to a bale of hay.

'There's nothing wrong with me!' insisted Grandpa, swaying from side to side. 'I just had a few glasses of nanny-goat brew.'

Fenda shook her head and placed Grandpa's right arm round her left shoulder. Eddie placed Grandpa's left arm round his right shoulder. Together they half-dragged/half-pulled him back to his sphere, with several Pembrans giving them funny looks on the journey.

As soon as they were home, Fenda fetched an enormous jug of iced gnat tea and poured it over Grandpa's head.

'WHAT DID YOU DO THAT FOR?' he yelled indignantly.

'You were outside the Bone and Beast singing about a Porcupig called Swirl,' said Fenda sharply.

'Was I?' asked Grandpa.

'The Porcupig died,' added Eddie.

'Oh dear,' said Grandpa, 'was its family very upset?'

'FORGET ABOUT THE IMAGINARY PORCUPIG!' snapped Fenda, 'I've had an idea.'

'Yes?' asked Grandpa, pouring gnat tea out of his right ear.

'I want to go and visit the Sage,' said Fenda. 'I have a feeling he might be able to help us.'

'You know that's not possible,' replied Grandpa, fixing a beady eye on his granddaughter.

'Why not?' demanded Fenda. 'He could be our last hope!'

'Number one, he's retired,' said Grandpa. 'Number two, he said he wasn't to be bothered again. Number three, rumour has it that he went completely batty some time ago. And number four – and this one is the most important – he lives on the other side of the Open Plains and as these are populated by large gangs of Grim

Grim Coyotes who like nothing better than devouring a tasty Pembran sandwich, YOU ARE NOT GOING!'

'Please, Grandpa! We can't just let the Vultrain brothers win. We'll have to face their gloating for the rest of our lives.'

'I'm sorry,' said Grandpa sternly, 'but it's too risky. You are not to go across the Open Plains and that's the end of it.'

Fenda sulked for the rest of the evening and whenever Grandpa said something to her she replied with a one-word answer. She went to bed straight after supper leaving Eddie and Grandpa to talk. Grandpa was fascinated by savoury crackers and Eddie had to explain all of the different types in the human world. It was late when they finally went to sleep.

*

Eddie was woken by a paw closing over his mouth. He was about to struggle when he realized it was Fenda's paw. A finger on her other paw was pressed to her lips. He nodded, she released her paw and together they tiptoed out of the sphere.

It was early morning and no one else was around.

'What are we doing?' asked Eddie.

'We're going to see the Sage,' whispered Fenda.

'But you heard what Grandpa said,' hit back Eddie, 'especially the bit about the Grim Grim Coyotes.'

'If we look menacing they probably won't touch us,' insisted Fenda, 'and anyway, we've hardly got any time left. Everyone says the Sage was always full of brilliant ideas and could solve any problems. He's only been retired five years – I'm sure he's still totally brainy and I just think we *have* to go and see him, whatever Grandpa says. Now are you coming or what?'

Eddie rubbed his eyes, partly from tiredness

and partly to try and bash his brain into giving Fenda an answer.

'OK,' he said after a few moments, 'I'm in. But Grandpa is going to KILL us, if the Coyotes don't get to us first.'

In the next twenty minutes they travelled down several passages, up three separate flights of steps and through six different doors, until they stood on the edge of a huge plain. The ground was covered by extra thick orange moss and this stuff wasn't warm, it was boiling; clouds of smoke were rising up from its surface.

Hundreds of tiny grey ants hurried over the moss in long formations, carrying strange-looking pink vegetables that were at least a hundred times as big as them. Very thin and tall zigzagged trees stood in various places on the landscape and there was a persistent buzzing sound in the air.

'That noise is made by packs of Coyotes,'

explained Fenda, 'but don't worry. It carries for miles.'

Eddie could only yelp as he stepped on to the moss, his feet suddenly sizzling. He jumped back off it.

'Stick some of this on the soles of your shoes,' said Fenda, chucking Eddie a roll of tape. 'It's heat resistant; we use it for travelling on hot ground.'

Eddie wrapped tape round the bottom of his shoes and Fenda wound some over her feet. Suddenly it was bearable to walk.

They set off at a brisk pace with an air of adventure and possibilities. They hadn't gone far when a large brown insect with a wasp-like head and a snake-like body flew straight towards Fenda's ears. In a flash she produced a giant fly swat and whacked the insect out of the way.

'Glum Flies,' she explained as the insect flew away in defeat. 'They live on Waxies.'

She produced a second swatter and handed it to Eddie.

For the next hour and a half they strode over the Open Plains, weaving past the thin trees and mashing any Glum Flies that came within mashing distance. They did spot a couple of Grim Grim Coyotes in the distance but they were alone and ran away when Fenda shouted at them. 'I told you,' she said, 'if they're not in a pack they're big-time cowards.'

As the clock hit the two-hour mark they finally saw a dwelling up ahead. It was a large sphere covered in white leaves. When they knocked on the door a small female Pembran with high cheekbones and a stoop opened the door.

She looked at them as if she hadn't had any visitors for months. 'We haven't had any visitors for months,' she said. 'How can I help you?'

'We're here to see the Sage,' said Fenda, 'it's really important.'

'I am Jodrel – his manservant,' said the female.

'How can you be his manservant when you're a woman?' asked Eddie.

Jodrel – the female manservant – ignored him and stayed silent.

'So, can we see him?' asked Fenda eagerly.

'Unfortunately no,' said Jodrel. 'He's gone away.'

'We can wait for him,' said Fenda. 'When is he back?'

Jodrel checked her watch and cleared her throat. 'In **three years**,' she replied.

'**THREE YEARS!**' shrieked Fenda.

'He's only just left though,' said Jodrel, 'and he doesn't go very fast. He went that way.'

Eddie and Fenda followed her finger and ran behind the sphere.

There, sitting on the back of a very old Porcupig who was going at about one mile per hour, sat the Sage with a serene smile on his face and a pair of earphones in his ears. He looked seriously old – much, much older than Grandpa – and had a long flowing green beard

which was wrapped several times around his neck like a scarf.

Fenda ran in front of the Porcupig and waved her arms for it to stop. This it did, but you could hardly notice the difference between when it was moving and when it was stationary. The Sage frowned and pulled the headphones out of his ears.

'I was just listening to one of the speeches

I made many years ago,' smiled the Sage. 'For some reason it sounds a lot like me.'

Eddie and Fenda exchanged a glance.

'Er ... my name is Fenda. My grandpa runs the old funfair in the valley,' said Fenda. 'And this is my human friend, Eddie.'

'The old funfair ...' mused the Sage, unwrapping his beard section by section until it stretched down to the ground. 'I remember going on its Zoom-a-Coaster as a boy.'

'That's the one!' said Fenda eagerly. 'Well, there's a big problem with the funfair and we were wondering if you could help us?'

'You want me to go on the Zoom-a-Coaster?' asked the Sage, now chewing the tip of his beard.

'No,' sighed Fenda, 'we need some financial help.'

'Hmmm,' said the Sage thoughtfully. 'I haven't had any connection with the settlement since my retirement, but I can give you a few minutes of my time.'

He climbed down off the Porcupig and slowly walked back to his sphere with Eddie and Fenda on either side. Jodrel's eyebrows danced in amazement at the sight of them stepping in together.

The inside of the sphere was filled with amazing sculptures and paintings in a variety of garish colours.

The three of them sat down and the Sage spoke first.

'So how can I help you with this new school then?' he asked.

'It's a funfair,' Fenda reminded him.

'Yes of course,' nodded the Sage. 'How can I help you with your recipe?'

'No, it's about the old FUNFAIR,' repeated Fenda, forcing herself to be patient with the ancient Pembran. 'We need to find a large sum of money to repair it or it will have to close forever and the Vultrain boys' new funfair will be the only show in town!'

'Financial help,' murmured the Sage thoughtfully, 'I think I might be able to help you there.'

Eddie and Fenda's eyes grew wide as the Sage got to his feet and slowly reached up to a small shelf. His fingers curled round an ancient-looking wooden box that had a coloured pattern on its outside – an exact copy of one of the paintings on the wall. He lifted it down carefully. 'This will most certainly help you in your quest,' he whispered, handing the box to Fenda.

Eddie felt a ripple of excitement over his entire body. *It's got to be cash – there could be thousands of Waxies in there!*

Fenda slowly opened the box and she and Eddie gazed inside at the contents.

'It's a nut,' said Eddie slowly, lifting up the small brown shell.

'Correct,' nodded the Sage, 'but it isn't just any type of nut, it's a Bumble Nut – the rarest and most delicious nut ever to have been found in these parts.'

'Er … how is this going to help us raise the money to save the funfair?' asked Fenda.

'It won't,' smiled the Sage, 'but it will give you something delicious to chew on while you're thinking about it.'

Fenda groaned quietly. Eddie closed his eyes for a few seconds and dropped the nut and the colourful box into his jacket pocket.

'Now I must be on my way,' said the Sage. 'I need to listen to a speech I gave many years ago, which …'

'… for some reason sounds like you,' offered Eddie.

'Exactly!' nodded the Sage. 'What a bright foreign creature you are!'

As the Sage prepared to restart his incredibly slow journey, Eddie and Fenda trudged out of his sphere and looked at the Open Plains stretching out in front of them.

'All of that travelling for a nut,' said Fenda with crushed disappointment. 'I should have listened to Grandpa.'

The high spirits of the outward journey were absent on the trek back and while the two of them swatted Glum Flies with enough power to send them packing, their footsteps were leaden and conversation was kept to a minimum. They were well over halfway back when Eddie spotted something up ahead.

'Oh no,' he muttered, pointing at a large gathering of sleek grey shapes.

Fenda followed his gaze and gulped anxiously. 'I don't think this lot will be put off by shouts and threats,' she observed.

Slowly the pack of Grim Grim Coyotes advanced towards them, slavering with anticipation, their amber eyes flashing.

Fenda unravelled her arms and waved them at the Coyotes.

'**LEAVE US ALONE!**' she yelled.

But the Coyotes were not deterred and slowly edged further and further forward until they'd formed a tight circle around their Pembran/human prey.

'Stand back!' said Eddie as he raised his arms
in the air, the Coyotes pressing ever further
forward.

Fenda's top eye spun several times around
her head. 'There's nowhere to go!' she shouted
as her and Eddie's backs were pressed against
each other at the centre of the circle.

'SHRINK YOURSELF!' commanded Eddie.
'I can handle them on my own.'

'Really?' gulped Fenda.

'Just do it!' ordered Eddie.

Fenda squeezed her nose, was reduced to a

tenth of her size and leapt in the air, landing briskly in Eddie's jacket pocket.

'TAKE THAT!' shrieked Eddie, suddenly lashing out with his arms and performing two terrifically fast and powerful kung-fu chops on the two Coyotes nearest him,

The attacked Coyotes flew backwards and howled in pain but another three lunged at Eddie. Spinning on his heels he caught all three of them with one forceful, sweeping side kick.

They reeled away. Another two attacked but he got them with powerful hand strokes.

The others stared at him with hunger and hatred but when he raised his arm again, the entire pack turned and fled, thundering over the Plains as fast as their sinewy legs would carry them.

'ULTRA FINE!' gasped Fenda, who had watched everything from the relative safety of Eddie's pocket. 'THAT WAS BRILLIANT!'

She jumped out, slapped her forehead and returned to her everyday size.

'All in a day's work,' grinned Eddie suavely.

Fenda laughed and they continued their walk, slightly buoyed by Eddie's defeat of the hungry grey beasts, but also weighed down by the *un*-success of their trip.

As they reached the end of the Plains, however, another frightening sight met them, but this time it wasn't Coyotes. Grandpa Zebu was standing there, his eyes red with anger.

'Uh oh,' whispered Fenda.

'You disobeyed me, Fenda!' he said gravely.

'I know, Grandpa, but we were on a mission!' huffed Fenda.

'And what did you achieve on this mission? Did you even see the Sage?'

'Yes,' replied Fenda defiantly, 'he invited us into his sphere!'

'Did he give you any Waxies?'

'Well, no, but …'

'So you placed yourselves in very great danger for nothing!' snapped Grandpa angrily. 'You could have been attacked by a large pack of Grim Grim Coyotes!'

'Actually … we were,' said Fenda.

'WHAT?' exploded Grandpa.

'It was way cool,' grinned Fenda. 'Eddie chopped and kung-fu kicked them away. You should have seen him!'

She mimicked Eddie's kung-fu moves.

'Incredible!' gasped Grandpa, who'd been

a big fan of Pembran martial arts in his youth.
When he started quizzing Eddie about his
kung-fu skills, Grandpa Zebu's anger quickly
evaporated, but as they approached his sphere
they were met by a most unwelcome sight.
Standing outside stood the Vultrain brothers,
grinning like they'd just won top prize in the
Pembran weekly lottery.

'What do you lot want?' snarled Fenda.

'We have a crucial document here,' answered Vix, unfurling a sheet of frayed parchment that he produced from the folds of his fur.

'This is an official declaration by the Pembran Powers that Be,' stated Vep seriously.

'Whatever the other two said,' chipped in Vad.

Vix turned the parchment round for Eddie, Fenda and Grandpa to see. They read it in silence.

WE THE POWERS THAT BE DO DECLARE IN RELATION TO GRANDPA ZEBU'S FUNFAIR THAT:

* EVERY PIECE OF EQUIPMENT AND EVERY RIDE MUST BE SAFE AND SECURE
* ALL MACHINERY MUST BE REPAIRED AND UPDATED APPROPRIATELY
* EVERY LOOSE CONNECTION AND SOCKET MUST BE PROPERLY AFFIXED

IF ANY OF THESE STEPS ARE NOT TAKEN BY 9 A.M. ON FESTIVAL DAY, THEN THE FAIR WILL BE DEEMED UNSAFE AND WILL BE IMMEDIATELY CLOSED. THERE IS NO RIGHT OF APPEAL ON THIS ORDER.

WE MEAN BUSINESS.

SIGNED - *the Powers That Be*

'Do you want us to start dismantling it *now*,' crowed Vix, 'seeing as you'll never be able to meet any of those requirements by 9 a.m. on Festival Day, which is, if you hadn't remembered … TOMORROW!'

'You lay one finger on it,' said Fenda, 'and I'll … I'll … I'll get Eddie to give you a blistering kung-fu chop!'

'Save your strength for pulling that old junk heap place apart!' giggled Vep.

Vix pushed the parchment into Grandpa's

hands and the three Vultrain Brothers skipped off, singing a song about how they now ruled the Pembran funfair world. Grandpa looked down at the parchment for a long time and then finally spoke.

'They're right,' he said softly, 'this really is the end. I'll get my spades and shovels and we'll begin taking it down right now.'

9

'No way, Grandpa!' shouted Fenda. 'There's still nearly fifteen hours till 9 a.m.'

'I know,' sighed Grandpa, 'and don't get me wrong – I'm very proud of you both for trying so hard, even though you ignored my specific instructions to stay off the Open Plains. But there's no point kidding ourselves. We haven't been able to raise sufficient funds and as time has all but run out, it really is over now.'

'But Grandpa …'

'No, Fenda,' said Grandpa Zebu sharply. 'If

you could take those shovels over there we'll get cracking.'

Fenda sighed and did as she was told.

It was a very forlorn party of three who arrived in the valley a short while later.

'OK, it's probably best to start with the arcade,' mused Grandpa. 'We'll unplug everything and then start cutting the machines out of their casings.'

'Please don't do this, Grandpa Zebu!' begged Fenda.

'I'm sorry,' said Grandpa, 'but there's no other way.'

Sensing he'd be required to do a large amount of physical work, Eddie emptied his pockets on to a small table. There was a set of keys, a pack of chewing gum, a football key-ring, the Bumble Nut and the small, colourful box.

'Where did you get that?' asked Grandpa, picking up the box to inspect it.

'The Sage gave it to us,' replied Fenda.

'Ah,' nodded Grandpa, 'you see the pattern on the outside of the box? That's copied from a Kubby Jonks painting.'

'Really?' asked Fenda. 'The Sage had loads of paintings like that on his walls. They looked like originals so they must be worth a fortune. Why don't we go back there and *borrow* one?'

Grandpa shot her a fierce look. 'Neither of you are going anywhere near the Open Plains again or there will be deadly serious trouble. Do you understand?'

They both nodded and Eddie could see from Fenda's expression that she wasn't prepared to disobey Grandpa again.

'Right,' said Grandpa briskly, 'to the arcade we go!'

They walked along the central path of the funfair, pausing to look up at the giant Zoom-a-Coaster for a few seconds. Eddie's eyes fixed on the multicoloured sign stating:

THE MONSTER WORLD'S FINEST
ZOOM-A-COASTER!
CAN YOU MAKE IT ROUND IN ONE PIECE?

He focussed on the letters, each constructed from different fragments of coloured wood.

As Eddie looked up, cogs, wheels and pistons suddenly cranked to life inside his brain.

'Hang on a minute,' he murmured.

'What is it?' asked Fenda.

Before she or Grandpa could stop him, Eddie grabbed an empty grey sack off the ground and started shinning up the bones of the Zoom-a-Coaster.

'GET DOWN AT ONCE!' shouted Grandpa, but Eddie pretended not to hear him. Higher and higher he climbed, nearly losing his footing on a couple of occasions, but a minute later he was standing on top of the

coaster, right beside the multicoloured letters.

Carefully he started picking off the pieces that made up the first letter – **T** – and dropped them into the grey sack.

'We're not going to start dismantling up there yet!' shouted Grandpa. 'The Zoom-a-Coaster's the last thing we'll bring down!'

'I won't be long!' shouted back Eddie, pulling free the pieces that made up the ' **H** '.

'What in the Sage's name is he doing?' murmured a bewildered Grandpa Zebu.

Fenda shrugged her shoulders.

By now Eddie was working feverishly away, dropping fragment after fragment into the grey sack. When he'd prised free every single piece, he began climbing down the coaster as fast as he could.

'What's going on?' demanded Fenda, staring at him in confusion.

'Just wait!' commanded Eddie, emptying the entire contents of the sack on to the ground.

'I know you mean well, Eddie,' huffed Grandpa, 'but we have a lot of work to do. Could you play your colourful little game a bit later?'

'It's not a game,' retorted Eddie, who was now moving the chunks around on the ground at great speed, while scratching his head and muttering to himself.

Grandpa started tapping his feet and whizzing his upper eye round his head impatiently. Fenda stood uncertainly with her paws on her hips. They were both about to move off when Eddie switched a large tranche of pieces round and suddenly a picture started taking shape – a picture that looked very familiar. It was of a tiny Pembran angel baby, playing a bone harp and sitting inside a bowl of fruit.

'What the …' gasped Fenda.

'Kubby Jonks DID leave you payment for his rent all those years ago!' said Eddie triumphantly, 'and THIS IS IT!'

Eddie pushed three more pieces into place and an image almost identical to the one on the box that the Sage had given to them was there on the ground.

'I don't get it,' said Fenda.

'Remember what you said, Grandpa Zebu?' cried Eddie. 'You said that when Kubby stayed with you, it was a time when *things were being built and taken apart all over the place.* He obviously left this painting for you as payment, but it was misplaced and someone – not knowing what it was – cut it up into pieces and used them for the Zoom-a-Coaster sign!'

Fenda and Grandpa stared at their human friend in silent astonishment.

'So I've been angry with him for all these years for no reason at all?' asked Grandpa.

Eddie nodded.

'Will the painting still be worth anything?' asked Fenda quickly.

'Well ... well ... yes!' cried Grandpa, 'it'll be worth a great deal!'

'Even though we'll have to stick the pieces together?' asked Eddie.

'Of course!' exclaimed Grandpa. 'In the same way that a human art collector would pay a vast sum if someone found say, an old Van Gogh painting in pieces, a Pembran Jonks fan would pay handsomely for this!'

'Do you know any Pembran art collectors?' asked Fenda, excitement suddenly flowing through her furry green body.

'As a matter of fact I do,' replied Grandpa. 'Old Grizzle Grench is a massive Jonks collector and he's fabulously wealthy.'

'Well give him a call,' shouted Eddie, 'we haven't got much time!'

So while Grandpa raced off to phone Grizzle Grench, Fenda went to get a large pot of glue from the fair store and Eddie finished putting all the pieces of Kubby Jonks's painting in the right places.

Thirty minutes later the picture had been glued together and the glue had dried. Fifteen minutes after that, Grizzle Grench came running down the hill carrying a large black suitcase made from Porcupig spikes.

'WHERE IS IT?' he shouted, racing towards them, '*WHERE IS IT?*'

As soon as he saw the painting he stopped dead in his tracks. 'Oh my word,' he said in a strangled whisper, 'it's from his lilac and tangerine period. This is ultra, ultra rare. I'll be the envy of Jonks collectors throughout the monster world.'

'What's in the case?' asked Fenda. Grizzle placed it down on the floor, twisted the combination lock and opened it. Inside was a massive collection of Waxies – more than Grandpa and Fenda had seen in their entire lives.

'Will that be enough to fix the funfair?' asked Eddie.

'It'll certainly allow us to give it a good go,' replied Grandpa, swaying slightly in shock.

'So we have a deal?' asked Grizzle.

'You bet!' nodded Fenda.

Zebu clenched his paws in delight and Eddie realized it was the first time since he'd been in the Pembran settlement that he'd seen Fenda's grandpa smile.

10

F estival Day dawned and there was a buzz of excitement throughout the Pembran settlement, nowhere more so than at the Vultrain brothers' brand-new funfair. The rides were gleaming, the arcades were spotless and the money-collecting buckets were huge.

'We are going to be RICH!' enthused Vix, rubbing his paws with glee.

'Pembrans will come from miles around to visit us!' crowed Vep.

'Whatever you two said,' nodded Vad.

The official opening time of the Vultrain

funfair was 9 a.m. and the three of them stood at the front entrance, fur brushed back, eyeballs shined and paws reaching out to take the first customers' cash.

But 9 a.m. came and went and the number of customers who arrived for the opening was … zero.

'They must have thought we said 9.30,' said Vix brightly.

But by 9.30 there were still no customers.

'They've all probably slept in as it's Festival Day,' reasoned Vep.

Ten o'clock came and went without any takers.

'Whatever you two said,' mouthed Vad.

When 10.30 passed, amid much grumbling, they decided to go and visit Grandpa Zebu's broken funfair, reasoning that their customers had probably gone there first and when they discovered how rubbish it was, they'd all come piling over to the Vultrain set-up.

It was with incredible shock then that as they reached the bottom of the hill leading up to the valley housing Grandpa Zebu's funfair they were caught up in a great throng of Pembrans, hurrying forwards with excitement dancing over their faces.

When the Vultrain boys reached the brow of the hill they looked down in stupefied silence. For there, instead of a funfair smouldering in its own smoky ruins, was a funfair gyrating in its pomp and splendour, with every ride dazzlingly repaired and updated, and thousands of customers already screaming in delight as they participated in the multiple attractions.

'How did he do it?' mouthed Vix as a big gang of Pembran kids elbowed him out of their way and ran cheering towards the fair.

'I don't know how he did it,' said Vep, 'but our fair is *just as good* as theirs. So why has everyone come here and no one showed at our place?'

'Because,' hissed Vix, who had spotted the

genius marketing trick, 'the ticket system here is slightly more attractive than our one.'

He pointed to the front entrance of the fair where Grandpa Zebu was issuing the tickets. As soon as a customer received their ticket they took it to a table where a large Pembran with a multicoloured waistcoat and matching hat drew a picture on it.

'Who's that?' asked Vep.

'That is none other than Mr Kubby Jonks!' seethed Vix. 'Every customer is getting a personalized Kubby Jonks illustration on their ticket! No wonder they're all flocking here and steering clear of our place!'

As soon as Grizzle Grench had handed the money over the night before, Grandpa Zebu had done two things. First, he'd called in every Pembran engineer, designer and builder and offered them treble wages if they could get the fair up and running to a mighty new standard by 9 a.m. the following morning. Secondly, he'd gone straight to Kubby Jonks's sphere and offered him a sincere apology for breaking off contact all those years ago.

When Kubby heard the story about his 'lost' painting and Grandpa had explained about the rival Vultrain fair, Kubby had suggested he draw on everyone's ticket to make each one a collector's item. Grandpa had been thrilled and had sent a Porcupig racing round the entire settlement broadcasting this news early that morning, a message unheard by the Vultrain boys because they'd been so obsessed with shouting at each other about how much money they were going to make.

And who was collecting the cash at Grandpa Zebu's funfair? A human named Eddie and a Pembran called Fenda. They were already on their third cash bucket each and were greeting every customer with chants and cheers and raucous songs.

A few minutes later, the dazed Vultrain brothers were standing on shaky legs next to Grandpa.

'Er ... is there any chance we could have our old jobs back?' asked Vix, squirming with shame and embarrassment. 'It's just that we borrowed a lot of money from Sproggy and the other loan sharks to get our fair going, and as we have no customers, we'll need to work pretty hard to pay them all back.'

Grandpa narrowed his eyes and looked them up and down. 'You may,' he finally said, 'on one condition.'

'Anything!' bleated the Vultrains.

'You don't open your fair here in the summer as competition to me, and in the winter, you take it on the road and visit all of the monster clans where there's never been a funfair before,' said Grandpa sternly. 'Do you agree to this?'

The Vultrains nodded their heads vigorously.

'Good,' nodded Grandpa, 'you're hired.'

And so, a short while later, the Vultrain brothers were scurrying round the Zoom-a-Coaster, sweeping and polishing the seats in the breaks between rides.

During one of these breaks, and unseen by the brothers, Eddie sneaked on to one of the coaster's seats, while Fenda raced over to press the START button and then dived back to land on the seat next to Eddie.

The Vultrain brothers were taken by surprise and as the coaster cranked into action, they had no choice but to grab hold of the seats they were cleaning.

'HELP!' screamed Vix.

'SAVE US!' shrieked Vep.

'WHATEVER THE OTHER TWO SAID!' bellowed Vad.

The Zoom-a-Coaster rapidly gained speed and Eddie pulled a small brown object out of his jacket pocket. He snapped the Bumble Nut in two and handed half to Fenda. They grinned at each other, popped their respective halves into their respective mouths and started chewing.

As the Coaster reached its highest point and the Vultrain brothers screamed and spluttered, Eddie and Fenda threw their arms in the air in complete agreement about one vital thing: the Sage had been right – the Bumble Nut *was* delicious!

FENDA
and the
FIERY CATERING FIASCO

Dear Eddie and family

I'm writing to say how grateful I am for you agreeing to host the visit of Fenda – a monster from the Pembran monster clan. Fenda is a very lively monster but as Pembrans have a five-foot girth she may find it hard to fit down the aisles of certain human shops. If she does get stuck, a great whack on the bottom with a tennis racket will generally push her through. Pembrans possess three eyes (the top one revolves all of the way around their heads) so it's generally best not to pull faces behind her back because she'll spot you. Fenda also has powerful springs on the underside of her feet so if she chooses  to leap over your house please don't be alarmed. However, it might be best to warn local pet owners to keep their animals inside to avoid them getting crushed when she lands. In addition, Fenda's great dream is to become a monster film star so if she tries to gobble up your camcorder she will only be doing it in the name of furthering her movie career. Finally, I can inform you that Fenda's arms can 'unravel' to great length so if you have a coin/toy/old sausage lodged somewhere behind the sofa, she will probably be able to get it out for you.

I wish you supremely good luck for Fenda's visit.

Yours sincerely

Sir Horace Upton

Human Agency for Understanding Monsters

1

Eddie walked up and down the pavement and tutted under his breath. It was a gorgeous summer day and the sunlight was bouncing off the glass storefronts dotted up and down the high street. Two young kids with their parents were walking by, with more ice cream on their faces than in their mouths.

Eddie paced some more.

Fenda had told him she wouldn't be arriving in the 'normal' way, but he had no idea what that meant. Would she jump out of a helicopter? Might she spring out of a streetlight? He was starting to fret; where was she? Maybe she'd gone to the wrong country.

But before he could take another anxious step, he heard a grinding noise and looked down to see a manhole cover in the middle of the road being slid aside by a ten-fingered green paw. The next second Fenda jumped out and waved excitedly at him. The ice-cream kids gazed at her in amazement; one dropped his ice cream on the other one's head.

'LOOK OUT!' screamed Eddie as a motor-bike hurtled round the corner. Fenda threw herself out of the way and the motorbike screeched past her, the driver staring in amazement at the leaping green creature.

'LOOK OUT AGAIN!' yelled Eddie as a bus crashed down the road, swerving and narrowly avoiding her.

Fenda skidded off the road and threw her arms round Eddie's stomach.

'You made it!' laughed Eddie, struggling for breath.

'Of course I did!' grinned Fenda, as she let go. 'I travelled mostly through your sewer system. But unlike in our one you have no refreshment stalls down there.'

Eddie was about to ask what kind of food seller would want to set up shop in a sewer, when Fenda grabbed his arm and started running down the street at a frantic pace.

'SHOW ME EVERYTHING, HUMAN!' she yelled, unable to contain her excitement. 'I want to see shoes, xylophones and especially banana yoghurt!'

Eddie raced along the high street with her, pointing out different items in the various shop windows and answering Fenda's rapid-fire questions.

'Is pizza a kind of toy?'

'Are a hoodie and a hoover the same thing?'

'Where are all the cheeseburger statues?'

After an extensive tour, Eddie finally managed to drag her away from the shops, across the park, and down several side roads, before arriving at his house, a tall white structure with sash windows and a white front door.

'This way,' he said, leading his new monster friend down a narrow passage at the side of the house. Fenda got stuck a couple of times on account of her five-foot width, but she pushed and twisted and completed the journey.

'Right,' said Eddie, when they'd made it to the back garden. 'First I want to teach you how to play football!'

'Ultra fine!' said Fenda.

'Your goal is here,' he said pointing to one net, 'and my goal is there,' he said pointing to another. 'The aim of the game is to score more goals than your opponent.'

'Cool!' nodded Fenda enthusiastically. She jumped into the air, bounced on top of the ball and flung *herself* into Eddie's net.

'**GOAL!**' cheered Fenda, wheeling away in delight.

'Er … it's not *you*, it's the ball …' tried Eddie, but Fenda was already jumping off the ball again and scoring another monster goal.

After a minute of trying to explain that Fenda had got it wrong, Eddie gave up and joined in with her rules. Half an hour later it was twenty Fendas to twenty Eddies – a suitably fair score.

In exhaustion, they lay down on their backs looking up at the royal-blue sky.

'The human world is excellent,' sighed Fenda contentedly. 'My mates back home will love your football game.'

'I'm back!' called a voice through an open window inside the house.

'Mum!' said Eddie, getting to his feet. 'This is Fenda!'

'Hello, Fenda,' said Eddie's mum, striding out into the garden, 'I'm so glad you got here safely!'

Eddie's mum was short and petite with long, straight black hair and large, smiling round eyes.

'Thanks for having me!' gushed Fenda, running up the garden and giving Eddie's mum such a fearsome stomach squeeze that they were both sent crashing over into a flowerbed.

'It's a pleasure,' croaked Mum gingerly, getting back to her feet.

'Humans are fascinating,' said Fenda, licking Mum's shoes.

'Actually, I'm glad you're both here,' said Mum. 'I made a new pudding earlier and I'd really like you to try it.'

Before they could answer, she dashed back inside the house.

'Pudding?' asked Fenda, whose diet consisted almost solely of a maroon plant which Pembrans grew on the outside of their sphere homes.

'My mum is trying to win the contract to make school dinners at Willow Street Primary School and she hasn't chosen a sweet food – a pudding – yet,' explained Eddie. 'There are two other people who want the contract and some food inspectors will choose which one of them wins the contract for the next twelve months.'

'How can we stop the others?' asked Fenda.

'We can't,' replied Eddie, 'they both cooked their sample meals last week. It's Mum's turn this Wednesday. She's come up with the main course – fluffy baked potatoes with fresh tomato and courgette sauce and a crisp green salad – but she hasn't found the right pudding yet.'

'**Voilà!**' trilled Mum, hurrying outside with a tray containing two brown and white discs.

'What are those?' asked Fenda.

'Chocolate and vanilla slices,' replied Mum. 'I think they may be the ones!'

Eddie and Fenda took one each and started eating, Fenda using her sweet tongue and keeping her savoury tongue for when needed.

'**YUK!**' cried Fenda, spitting her slice all over the grass.

'You don't like it?' asked Mum, looking crestfallen.

'It's **DISGUSTING!**' beamed Fenda.

'Don't worry, Mum,' said Eddie. 'Pembrans only eat rich dessert foods on special occasions, like birthdays, so most sweet things will probably taste frightful to Fenda.'

'You got it in one!' grinned Fenda, taking another bite and showering the grass with more crumbs.

'What about you, Eddie?' asked Mum anxiously. 'Do *you* like it?'

'If I'm honest, Mum,' said Eddie chewing slowly, 'I don't think this *is* the one. It's OK but not great.'

'Oh dear,' said Mum, looking wounded. 'If I don't think up something fast I won't be able to do my sample meal on Wednesday and I'll never win that contract.'

She turned and walked forlornly back towards the house.

'Don't worry,' Eddie called after her, 'you'll think of something.'

But judging by her furrowed brow and pinched cheeks, it was clear she didn't share any of her son's confidence.

2

'Come on,' said Eddie. 'I want to show you my room.'

He and Fenda ran inside, through the kitchen – where Mum was trawling through a cookbook – up the stairs and into Eddie's bedroom. It was square with a bed in the far left corner, a wardrobe in the right and posters of great footballers, basketball players and kung-fu fighters splashed all over the walls. On top of a chest of drawers was a mountain of puzzles ranging in level from 'Easy' to 'Fiendish'.

'Look over there,' said Eddie proudly, 'I've made you your own perch.'

He pointed at two jutting out bars of wood he'd affixed to the wall, for Fenda to sleep on, because Pembrans slumbered like bats – upside down.

'Ultra fine!' grinned Fenda appreciatively.

'This is the one thing I couldn't live without!' said Eddie, holding up his games console – a rectangular black panel with a smallish screen and lots of colourful buttons. Fenda snatched it from his hands and popped it into her mouth.

'WHAT ARE YOU DOING?' screamed Eddie, diving towards her and pulling it out before she gulped it down.

'Oh sorry,' grinned Fenda, 'back home, we have games that you swallow. It allows you to really get *inside* the game … or at least, let the game get inside you.'

'Eddie!' called Mum, 'I'm just going to have

a soak in the bath to see if I can dream up the perfect pudding.'

'Cool, Mum!' called back Eddie, while Fenda started pacing around his bedroom, picking things up – a globe, an atlas, a pair of roller blades – examining them and then chucking them over her shoulder. Eddie had to dive out of the way several times to avoid being struck by one of these objects.

'You know what,' said Fenda thoughtfully, lobbing an encyclopaedia towards Eddie's head, 'I reckon *I* might be able to help your mum.'

'You want to run the bath for her?' asked Eddie.

'No,' said Fenda, 'I've just thought about a cookery class we did at school where we made a classic Pembran birthday pudding. It's one sweet food that Pembrans find delicious! I can't remember the exact ingredients but I know enough to have a go.'

'But would *humans* like it?' asked Eddie hesitantly.

'Like it?' grinned Fenda. 'They'll LOVE it! They'll want seconds and thirds and fifteenths!'

'I don't know,' said Eddie, chewing his bottom lip.

'Come on!' pleaded Fenda. 'I'll make it while your mum's in the bath. By the time she gets downstairs it'll be waiting for her on the kitchen table and all of her pudding worries will be over!'

'Well … OK,' replied Eddie reluctantly, 'she *is* getting a bit desperate and maybe something exotic could do the trick.'

'Excellent!' cried Fenda running to the door with Eddie close behind.

Downstairs Fenda started collecting ingredients: yeast, sugar, blackcurrant jam, sprinkles, five tulips from the garden, fizzy lemonade, tartar sauce, a roll of newspaper, two handfuls of grass, a large unpeeled onion and a bottle of tomato ketchup with no ketchup in.

'Are you *sure* you know what you're doing?' asked Eddie nervously.

'Relax,' grinned Fenda. 'Watch the pudding maestro at work!'

She chucked large amounts of everything into Mum's mixer and hit the **ON** switch. The mixer made a noise that it had never made before and steam started shooting out of its spout, but when Eddie took an anxious step closer to the machine, Fenda flicked him away. When she was done Eddie found himself looking down at a bright pink mixture. Fenda grabbed a dish and spooned the mixture into it.

'It looks a bit ... you know ... weird,' commented Eddie, trying to be tactful. 'Will it be *safe* to eat?'

'Of course!' laughed Fenda. 'Now, have you got some kind of heating-up machine?'

'There's the oven,' said Eddie, 'but the microwave is quicker.'

'I reckon we should use the microwave then,' said Fenda.

'OK,' nodded Eddie, 'but for ten minutes maximum.'

'That should be plenty of time,' agreed Fenda.

Eddie took the dish and placed it inside the microwave. He shut the door, hit a few buttons and the dish began to rotate slowly.

'Brilliant!' grinned Fenda, her nose pressed up against the glass door. 'The kids at your school are in for a delectable surprise when your mum does that meal! She's bound to win the contract after they've tasted this!'

After a minute the mixture began gently bubbling and frothing inside the dish.

Eddie frowned.

After two minutes, it was moving a bit more powerfully and started rising to the top of the dish.

Eddie winced.

After three minutes … the dish exploded.

Fortunately, Eddie and Fenda managed to dive on to the floor a split second before shards of glass, plastic and pink mixture were sent flying all over the kitchen.

They stood a few moments later.

'**DISASTER!**' groaned Eddie, surveying the quite spectacular carnage.

'I must have added too much yeast!' mused Fenda, climbing up on to one of the surfaces and spooning some mixture into her mouth

with her paw. 'For my second batch, I'll use less.'

'There won't be a second batch!' exclaimed
Eddie. 'If we don't get this mess cleared up soon
my mum is going to kill us!'

'Are you two OK down there?' called Mum
from the bathroom, having heard a dull thud and
some sort of crashing sound from downstairs.

'We're … we're absolutely fine!' shouted back
Eddie, grabbing a broom and madly starting to
sweep up. 'We're just watching TV.'

'OK,' said Fenda with disappointment. She got on her paws and knees and began picking up rubbish with her sweet tongue and depositing it in the bin with her savoury tongue.

'Hurry up!' hissed Eddie. 'We're never going to be finished in time!'

And sure enough, five minutes later when Mum's footsteps sounded on the stairs, the kitchen still resembled a zombie/alien bomb site.

'Delay her, Fenda!' ordered Eddie desperately, shooing his monster associate out of the kitchen.

'Can I just show you my impressions from back home?' asked Fenda as Mum reached the bottom of the stairs and found her way blocked.

'Sure,' said Mum, sitting on the bottom stair while Fenda impersonated a Pembran-monster-carrying Porcupig, a Grim Grim Coyote and Mr Flabberkins, her exceptionally thin art teacher.

'How fascinating,' said Mum, clapping and getting to her feet. Fenda tried to stop her but Mum nipped past Fenda and stepped into the kitchen. Fenda ran in behind her, terrified of the scene that would be awaiting her.

But the kitchen was absolutely spotless.

'It smells a bit funny in here,' said Mum suspiciously, reaching out to open a window. 'You haven't been doing any cooking, have you?'

'*Cooking!*' blurted out Eddie with a false laugh. 'Why on earth would we do *that?*'

'Yeah,' scoffed Fenda, 'it's not like I'd try and make a Pembran dessert with whatever ingredients were available, end up using too much yeast and in the process blow up the—'

Eddie slapped a hand over Fenda's mouth.

'Mhzvfyufnth!' said Fenda.

Mum pursed her lips and for a minute Eddie thought she was about to scream at them. Luckily though, she was focussing so intently on getting ideas for her pudding that she didn't notice the massively bulging dustbin, nor the large gap on the surface where the microwave oven had stood for the last six years.

3

'Evening, everyone!' came a loud voice from the hallway.

'It's Dad!' shouted Eddie, grabbing Fenda by the arm and dragging her out of the kitchen.

Eddie's father had changed out of his fire fighter's overalls at work, and was now wearing jeans, a white T-shirt and a light grey beanie hat. He had thick white hair and kind green eyes. He took off his hat and with delight cried, 'YOU MUST BE FENDA!'

He went to shake her paw but she avoided his hand and gave him one of her crushing-round-your-belly hugs.

When Dad had extricated himself from her grasp he half-wheezed/half-laughed, 'Eddie warned me about your hugs – I should have remembered!'

'You're a real human fireman!' grinned Fenda. 'How ultra fine is that? Can I drive your fire engine please?'

'Unfortunately no,' replied Dad, 'but thanks for the offer.'

Fenda looked a bit down-hearted, but Eddie put his arm round her shoulder. 'Don't worry,' he said, 'he never lets me drive it either.'

The three of them walked into the kitchen.

'I'll do supper,' announced Dad.

'Would you?' asked Mum feverishly, a cookery book in each hand. 'That would be wonderful!'

So half an hour later they sat down at the kitchen table and tucked into large portions of Dad's spaghetti bolognese. Fenda was a bit suspicious of the spaghetti at first – attacking the strands with her knife as if they were evil worms – but after taking a few mouthfuls, she decided she liked it and began shovelling it in.

Over supper, Dad told them about the fire he and his crew had put out in a block of flats that afternoon, Mum talked about her lack of pudding ideas and Fenda told them about her ambition to become a monster film star. 'I only want to be in movies where I get to kick monster butt,' she explained between mouthfuls. 'And I want to drive a monster sports car off the edge of a cliff but be saved by wrapping my tongues around a tree branch!'

'Sounds exciting,' said Dad. 'Who is your monster film hero?'

'Banty Globule is the greatest monster actress of all time!' enthused Fenda. 'She can vaporize baddies with one sharp look from her roaming upper eye!'

Fenda spun her top eye right round her head to demonstrate.

'Excellent!' laughed Eddie.

Following the spaghetti they had some fruit and when Dad had cleared the plates away, Mum made an announcement. 'It's time to watch the DVD again. I want everyone to know exactly what's involved in the sample meal, as you'll all be helping in your own ways.'

'Do we have to?' groaned Eddie. 'We've seen it a zillion times.'

But Mum fixed him with a stare that would have made Banty Globule proud, before putting a DVD into the player on the work surface and flicking on the kitchen TV.

The faces of two people appeared on the screen. The first was a short man with a long drooping moustache and rosy cheeks. The second was a tall, wiry woman with small, suspicious eyes and a nose like a mini-version of a toucan's beak.

'Greetings, potential lunchtime contractor,' said the man, looking into the camera with a beady eye. 'My name is Mr Cheeves.'

'And I'm Miss Briskit,' said the woman.

'We are the inspectors who will be visiting and assessing your sample lunch at your chosen school,' said Mr Cheeves.

'We are strict and we are thorough,' said Miss

Briskit, 'we know our onions from our avocados.'

'And our cutlery from our cake-bread,' added Mr Cheeves.

There followed a ten-minute lecture on health and safety regulations that had to be observed in school kitchens. Mum took notes throughout this lecture even though she'd seen it a dozen times before.

'We trust that all of these regulations will be observed,' said Miss Briskit curtly.

Mum nodded at the screen.

'That leaves us with two final matters,' said Mr Cheeves.

'Number one,' said Miss Briskit, 'you must keep to the allocated budget and may not spend a penny more.'

'And number two,' said Mr Cheeves, 'your time-keeping must be perfect.'

'The school lunch hour unsurprisingly lasts one hour,' said Miss Briskit, 'and we place very great importance on you starting to serve, stopping serving, and removing all diners by the stipulated times.'

'Failure to stick to this very strict timetable will mean failure for you,' added Mr Cheeves sternly.

'We look forward to seeing you shortly,' nodded Miss Briskit.

The screen went blank.

'Right,' said Mum, 'let's go over the master plan.' She grabbed her pad and consulted it. Eddie shook his head in despair.

'Tomorrow you three will get all of the household items from the supermarket and I'll make a final decision about puddings,' began Mum. 'Eddie and Fenda will then design and make all the menus and posters.'

'**CHECK!**' said Eddie and Dad.

'On Monday morning those menus and posters will go up in school.'

'**CHECK!**' said Eddie, Dad and now Fenda.

'On Tuesday afternoon I will buy all of

the baking potatoes and then at about six I'll go to Rita's fruit and veg place and buy all the tomatoes, lettuce and courgettes at the special price she's offered me.'

'**CHECK!**' responded the three listeners.

'On Wednesday, I'll get into school early to set up the kitchens. At morning break Eddie and Fenda will come and join me and we'll put the finishing touches to everything. You two will then help me serve.'

'**CHECK!**'

'After that it's in the hands of the inspectors. Is everyone clear about their role?'

Eddie and Dad nodded.

'**CHECK!**' said Fenda.

'Good,' said Mum, sweeping out of the room, clutching her pad to her chest and muttering pudding ideas to herself.

Dad started washing up. 'Will one of you dry please?' he asked.

'**CHECK!**' said Fenda, drying a plate on her fur.

Dad handed her a tea towel. 'It might be better if you use this,' he suggested.

'**CHECK!**' replied Fenda.

'You can stop saying check,' said Eddie.

'**CHE**—' said Fenda, stopping herself.

When the washing and drying was over and Eddie had put away all of the plates and cutlery, Dad pulled a face. 'Where's the microwave?' he asked.

'Oh … er … Mum … er … got rid of the old one,' said Eddie. 'She wanted to see if you'd spot it was missing and work out she wanted a new one.'

'Yeah,' nodded Fenda, 'she said there was no way you'd notice it was gone.'

'Really,' asked Dad, which could have meant:

a) I *totally believe you.*

OR

b) Why are you telling me such a whopping lie and what really happened to the microwave?

But Eddie didn't really want to hang around to find out which one Dad meant.

So he grabbed Fenda by the elbow and sped back up to his room.

4

'This water tastes horrible!' shouted Fenda, taking a long drink from the paddling pool in the back garden. It was a gorgeous Sunday afternoon and all down the street you could hear kids playing outside.

'That's because you're not *meant* to drink it!' cried Eddie, running down the garden to stop her.

Fenda spun out of his way and tripped him up so that he went flying headfirst into the pool. Eddie emerged from the water completely drenched but he made a quick lunge for Fenda's savoury tongue and pulled her in too.

The next hour was spent doing water kung-fu kicks and covering each other with tidal wave splashes.

When Dad called out of the window that soon it would be time to go to the supermarket, Eddie ran inside to get a couple of towels. When he got back out he saw Fenda unravelling her arms to five times their usual length and picking up the entire paddling pool before emptying it over the fence into the Crumpsalls' garden next door, while knocking down part of the fence in the process.

Unfortunately, Mr Crumpsall was attending to his roses right next to the fence so he got covered by the biggest tidal wave of all, and it took Eddie and Dad some considerable time to explain to him that Fenda was a monster and therefore didn't know about not-soaking-your-neighbours etiquette, and to promise him they'd mend the fence that day.

They piled into the car and a short while later Dad pulled in to the retail park. 'OK,' he said, 'I need to go to the hardware store to get some wood to fix the fence. You two go to the supermarket and buy the stuff on Mum's list.'

He handed Eddie a piece of paper and some money. The list stated:

- 10 x *rolls* of kitchen foil
- 8 x *rolls* of cling film
- 2 x containers of multi-purpose kitchen spray
- 6 x thick and absorbent kitchen *roll*

The supermarket was very busy, mainly with mothers and fathers hissing at their children to put back twelve-packs of chunky chomp bars they'd slipped into the trolley, and the odd harassed-looking worker hiding in case someone asked them where the grated cheese was.

Eddie grabbed a trolley and for the first few minutes, he and Fenda took turns – one pushing the trolley, the other clinging on to its underside and travelling a few centimetres above the floor.

'The signs above the aisles tell you where things are,' explained Eddie.

'That's such a good idea!' enthused Fenda. 'In our supermarkets everything is just piled on top of everything else and it's a miracle if you ever find what you're looking for.'

'OK,' nodded Eddie a few moments later, pulling to a halt. 'This is where the tin foil is.'

He looked at the bottom of the trolley but Fenda was nowhere to be seen.

'Fenda?' he called.

A second later a pack of tin foil hit him on the left shoulder and bounced into the trolley. He looked up and saw that Fenda had shrunk herself to a tenth of her usual size, shot up on to the shelves and was now lobbing kitchen foil grenades at him. Another pack came crashing down. He snatched at it and lobbed it into the trolley.

But the next one was falling some distance away and he had to run with the trolley to catch it. The next seven rolls came pelting down in different places so he had to whizz up and down the aisle in a desperate attempt to grab them.

By sheer speed and quick thinking, he got all ten in the trolley instead of letting them hit little children on the head.

'Fenda, I think we should . . .'

But Fenda had already moved down the aisle and had started on the cling film. The first roll was about to hit a very large man with a skull and crossbones tattoo on his neck, so Eddie ditched the trolley, raced down the aisle and leapt into the air to catch it.

'Nice one!' nodded the tattoo man.

But Eddie couldn't rest on his laurels because another seven cling-film rolls were soon raining down and in true goalkeeper style, he flung himself this way and that to catch them, before adding them to the trolley.

Next, Fenda was chucking two multi-purpose kitchen sprays like spears and Eddie was very lucky to catch one in each hand.

Then she disappeared again.

Eddie grabbed his trolley and began racing towards the aisle where the kitchen roll was situated. Fenda had beaten him to it though and she was standing on top of the shelf, hurling packs of kitchen roll down in the direction of several customers. These alarmed shoppers screamed and raced off to get the manager, but an elderly man wearing an orange cap at a jaunty angle was whacking the packs back at Fenda, using a large box of dog food as a bat.

Eddie reached up, grabbed Fenda in his left hand and with his right hand pulled down three double packs of kitchen roll.

He placed Fenda on the floor. She slapped herself on the forehead and in a flash was back to her normal size.

'Ohhhh!' she complained. 'That was SO fun.'

'Yeah!' shouted the dog food batsman. 'I was just getting into my stride!'

'Sorry but the game's over,' said Eddie, quickly steering Fenda and the trolley down the aisle to the checkout tills.

'I'm coming here again!' cried Fenda excitedly.

I'm not, thought Eddie.

The man on the till looked at Fenda for a few seconds, thinking perhaps she was an early Hallowe'en costume and should be scanned, but when she started talking he quickly changed his mind.

As Eddie paid he heard a chorus of voices behind him shouting, 'THERE'S THAT KITCHEN ROLL-THROWING BEAST!'

Eddie looked round and saw a gaggle of shoppers accompanied by the store manager – a large man with a very sweaty brow – running towards the tills.

'MOVE, FENDA!' he hissed.

Towards the exit they ran, the manager and his shoppers taking a different route.

'They're going to cut us off,' said Fenda.

As Eddie and Fenda neared the doors, so did their pursuers. In a moment of panic and seeing a gigantic display of cereal packets, Eddie 'by accident' shot out his foot and sent the entire mountain cascading down on to the hapless manager and his shopper army.

The next second he and Fenda were outside, haring over to the car. Dad was waiting inside. Eddie and Fenda threw the items they'd bought into the boot and dived inside the car.

'DRIVE!' commanded Eddie.

'What's with the rush?' enquired Dad.

'Nothing,' replied Eddie, looking round and seeing the manager and his groupies bearing down on the car, some of them with cereal packets still on their heads. 'I just can't wait to show Mum all of this kitchen stuff!'

'OK,' nodded Dad, gunning the engine and

driving off, a split second before the pursuers reached them.

'How did it go inside the supermarket?' asked Dad, pulling on to the main road. 'Any problems?'

'It was ultra fine!' beamed Fenda. 'Particularly the dog food man!'

Dad shot Fenda a quizzical look.

'It was totally straightforward,' said Eddie through gritted teeth. 'No problem at all.'

5

'Have you seen the microwave?' asked Mum when Eddie and Fenda entered the kitchen. Dad had gone to the garage to cut his wood into the right lengths to mend the garden fence. There were loads of cookery books and newspaper clippings all over the kitchen table and surfaces, covered with pictures of different puddings.

'Er ... Dad ... er ... said microwaves are dangerous so he took it to the recycling dump,' said Eddie.

'Yeah,' added Fenda, 'all of those crazy

cooking rays! He said he was going to get an ecologically-sound one.'

Mum frowned at them but her mind quickly returned to cooking. 'Did you remember to get a wooden spoon?' she asked.

'There wasn't one on the list,' replied Eddie.

Mum sighed deeply. 'I think my one fell down the back of the drawers,' she said, pulling at a unit until it moved out. Her wooden spoon was on the floor but it wasn't that which grabbed Eddie and Fenda's attention. Stuck to the wall behind the drawers was a large splat of Fenda's gooey pink mixture.

'What on earth is that that?' asked Mum suspiciously.

Before Eddie and Fenda could intervene, Mum scooped some up with a finger, smelt it and then licked it. Her expression suddenly transformed from glum to enthralled.

'IT TASTES OF PLUMS!' she shouted. 'THAT'S THE ANSWER!'

'There were no plums in the Pembran pudding,' mused Fenda, but Mum wasn't listening. She quickly checked her watch. 'The supermarket is still open,' she said in a frenzied tone. 'If I'm quick I'll be able to get some plums and do a trial run!'

And with that she raced out of the kitchen, put on her coat and snatched up the car keys. She was back within twenty minutes and an hour later she made a fanfare and pulled several trays of mini plum puddings out of the oven.

'TRY THEM!' she commanded.

Eddie, Fenda and Dad all bit into one of the maroon and brown delicacies.

'WELL?' demanded Mum.

There was silence in the kitchen for a few moments and then the judges' verdicts started coming in.

'You know what,' said Eddie, 'they're ... AMAZING!'

'DELICIOUS!' agreed Dad.

'REALLY GOOD!' nodded Fenda, only spitting out a couple of crumbs.

'YES!' screamed Mum, hugging all three of them. 'That's sorted! Plum pudding is our dessert!'

'Ultra fine!' beamed Fenda.

'You need to get ready for work,' said Mum to Eddie's dad, 'and now we know what the pudding is, you two need to crack on with the posters and menus,' she instructed Eddie and Fenda.

'I'll hopefully be back by midnight because I'm on shift again tomorrow morning at eight,' Dad notified all present before getting his stuff and heading off.

The gloom that had been lingering in the kitchen like the smell of burnt fish ever since the pudding dilemma had landed was now miraculously lifted and Eddie and Fenda set about their task with great zeal and delight.

Eddie brought down reams of paper and tins of coloured felt-tip pens and crayons. He also flicked on the laptop in the sitting room and the two of them produced sheet after sheet of computer-generated and old-fashioned pen-generated menus and posters advertising Mum's sample meal.

They were on poster number twenty-five when the phone went in the hallway.

'I'll get it!' called Mum, nipping out of the kitchen.

They heard Mum's voice suddenly go very

loud and then immediately tail off to a whisper. They looked at each other in confusion.

Three seconds later Mum staggered into the kitchen, the phone held limply in her right hand. She was so ashen-faced her cheeks were almost see-through.

'What's up, Mum?' asked Eddie, looking at her with concern.

'That … that was Mr Cheeves, the food inspector,' she replied in a voice so quiet it was only just possible to hear her.

'What did he want?' enquired Fenda.

Mum slumped down into an armchair. 'He and Miss Briskit have been told they have to do some sort of special emergency inspection at a community centre on Wednesday so they can't inspect my lunch then.'

'So they've cancelled your sample meal and put it back to Thursday or Friday, right?' demanded Eddie.

Mum shook her head.

'To next week?' asked Fenda.

'No,' replied Mum hoarsely, 'they've brought it forward.'

'Forward!' thundered Eddie. 'They can't do that!'

'Yes they can,' murmured Mum.

'So you have to do it on Tuesday?' asked Fenda.

'No,' replied Mum miserably. 'I have to do it tomorrow!'

6

'TOMORROW!' shrieked Eddie and Fenda in unison.

'That's right,' nodded Mum. 'That's the only slot Mr Cheeves and Miss Briskit have left in their schedule. He said if I felt I couldn't do it at such short notice then that's OK, he'd understand, but I'd have to wait twelve months until the contract comes up for renewal again.'

'So what did you say?' demanded Eddie.

'I asked him to give me some time to think about it, but I've made my mind up: I'm going to say no.'

'You can't say no!' said Fenda. 'You're the queen of catering!'

'Thank you, Fenda,' said Mum, managing a half smile.

'But surely you can get it together if we help you?' said Eddie. 'We could stay up all night!'

'That's very kind of you,' replied Mum, 'but I'll never be able to get hold of the ingredients in time. I could get the potatoes from Mr Raj's shop on the corner and I've probably got enough ingredients to make the right amount of plum puddings, but there's no way I could lay my hands on the fresh tomatoes, courgettes and salad stuff because Rita's shop is closed now and she doesn't open on Mondays.'

'Why don't you just get it from the supermarket tomorrow morning?' asked Fenda.

'Because I'll go over budget,' grimaced Mum. 'Rita's prices are the only way I can do it. I'm sorry you two but I'm going to phone Mr Cheeves back and say I'm out for this year.'

Mum suddenly looked smaller and sadder than Eddie had ever seen her. It was while he was looking at her that a thought suddenly leapfrogged into his brain.

'Hang on,' he said slowly, 'I've got an idea.'

'Do we kidnap Rita and demand some courgettes as a ransom?' asked Fenda excitedly.

'No,' replied Eddie, 'it's about Uncle Dan's allotment. I was there recently and he has bundles of tomatoes and carrots and lettuce and stuff.'

Mum smiled. 'That's a lovely idea,' she sighed, 'but Dan's on holiday in Spain at the minute and he won't be back till next weekend. And anyway, he couldn't let us take half of his produce.'

'You never know,' said Eddie. 'Why don't you phone him?'

'No, Eddie.'

'Well if you won't, I will,' said Eddie firmly. But dialling Uncle Dan's phone just got a message that it was unavailable at the moment.

'Please, Mum,' said Eddie, putting the phone down, 'he won't mind if we borrow some stuff, and we can pay him back in seeds and things.'

Mum shook her head wearily.

'What Eddie is saying makes sense,' said Fenda. 'Can you imagine what it will be like to have to wait a whole year before you can try again? Plus, if you pull out, one of the other two people will win it and they might do such a good job that the inspectors decide to keep them on automatically, and then you'll be blocked out of the entire thing.'

'Good point!' nodded Eddie, squeezing Fenda's shoulder.

Mum took a very deep breath and blew out her cheeks. 'You do have a point, Fenda,' she conceded.

'Come on, Mum!' urged Eddie.

'I don't like it,' said Mum, 'but maybe it is worth a try. But you'll have to do it without me

because I've got so much stuff to prepare here
… just in case we're still on.'

'We're definitely still on,' nodded Fenda.

Ten minutes later Eddie and Fenda were
ready. They were both wearing black – Eddie
in black jeans and sweatshirt, Fenda in one of
Eddie's black hoodies and a pair of Mum's black
tights. Fenda also insisted on wearing a pair
of Dad's oversized sunglasses. Eddie held the

camping torch in his hand and had two massive shopping bags draped over his shoulder.

'If it's too hard to get in there, forget it and come straight home,' ordered Mum as they stood on the doorstep. 'I don't want either of you being garrotted by razor wire.'

'It's an allotment, Mum, not a high security prison,' replied Eddie.

'It's completely crazy,' said Mum, 'but off you go.'

Eddie and Fenda raced outside and were swallowed up by the shadows.

Down the street, across the main road, past the dry cleaner's and the post office, along the crumbling path beside the old railway and finally to the fence enclosing the thirty strips of land that made up the allotments.

Behind the allotments was the Common – a large field where people walked their dogs and kids played football. Several distant lights were coming from the far end of the Common, but Eddie and Fenda didn't notice them.

Their focus was solely on the veg.

Eddie grabbed the metal fence and shinned to the top, lowering himself over and landing with a thud on a patch of grass on the other side. Fenda simply squeezed her nose, shrank herself and walked through one of the fence's

wiry criss-crosses. Eddie flicked on the torch, Fenda re-sized and they crept over to Uncle Dan's patch.

Eddie tied the torch to a wooden pole, illuminating the rows and rows of vegetables and fruit that Dan cultivated so lovingly. 'OK,' said Eddie, handing one of the large sacks to Fenda. 'You pick the tomatoes – those red things there – off their plants; I'll grab the courgettes and lettuces. Then we'll get out of here.'

'**CHECK!**' nodded Fenda. 'I mean … yes!'

She knelt down on the damp grass and starting picking tomatoes off their vines and stuffing them into her sack. They were plump and juicy but she didn't take any bites … at least, not that many. Eddie tiptoed to the neat lines of lettuces and began lifting them from their roots and bagging them.

Neither of them noticed that the lights on the Common were getting bigger by the second and were advancing silently towards the allotments.

When Eddie had bagged a sizeable number of lettuces he moved on to the courgettes. He was just finishing these off when Fenda hissed, 'I'm done!'

'Brilliant!' nodded Eddie.

He grabbed the torch and quickly tied up the two sacks with lengths of twine he'd taken from the kitchen drawer. Springing back on to the fence he motioned for Fenda to pass him the first sack, which she did. He climbed over and dropped down the other side, carefully placing the sack down on the ground. He went back for the second sack and repeated this procedure.

'Now you,' he whispered to Fenda.

Once again, Fenda reduced her size and slipped through the fence, re-inflating on the other side.

'Great work!' grinned Eddie at his allotment-entering partner.

But in their glow of satisfaction, neither of

them saw that the lights from the Common had now snaked down by the side of the allotments.

And with a great cry of '**GET THEM**' the holders of those lights suddenly pounced.

7

Eddie looked up just in time to see a large group of scouts and their leader come flying towards him and Fenda. They had been doing a camp-out on the Common when they'd detected noises coming from the allotments. And as the scouts were agents of all that is good, honest and doesn't lie about brushing its teeth, they had decided to investigate.

'**THIEVES!**' yelled the scouts.

Eddie *could* have given them a short lecture about the fact that the vegetables in the sacks belonged to his Uncle Dan. And he *could* have

attacked them with kung-fu moves. But the
scouts didn't look as if they were in the mood
for explanations; it looked like they really, really
wanted to catch some criminals.

So Eddie and Fenda did the next best thing;
they legged it.

'**SCOUNDRELS!**' screamed the scouts,
racing after them.

Eddie and Fenda sped down past the railway and instead of turning on to the main road, they skidded to the left, raced under a bridge, spun past the library and rushed round the corner, diving through a gap in a hedge that was well known to Eddie as he'd used it as a hiding place several times before.

'**WHERE ARE THEY?**' demanded the scouts, bursting round the corner.

'**SPREAD OUT!**' commanded their leader, hoping to catch the thieves red-handed and thus get a favourable mention both within the scout movement and in the local newspaper which was read by all of his friends and family.

'How about through here?' shouted one of the scout army, stepping through the gap in the hedge. He looked left and saw nothing. He looked right and drew a blank. If he'd looked up he would have seen Eddie and Fenda lying on a very narrow ledge next to a sloping garage roof. The scout muttered something to himself and retreated back through the hedge.

Eddie and Fenda waited until every scout's footstep had drifted away and then waited a bit more, before finally climbing down and cautiously peeking through the hedge into the street.

It was deserted.

'What would they have done to us if they'd caught us?' asked Fenda.

'They'd probably have made us help an old lady cross a road,' replied Eddie.

'Weird punishment,' replied Fenda. 'In my clan you'd probably get one of your tongues tied round your head for the rest of the week.'

Eddie winced and stealthily they crept back home.

Mum gasped when they emptied their sacks on to the kitchen table. 'This is AMAZING work!' she said, trying to keep calm. 'No one saw you, did they?'

'No,' replied Eddie.

'And if they had they'd only have made us help an old lady cross a road,' added Fenda.

Mum gave Fenda a quizzical look and then asked her and Eddie to start slicing courgettes. 'We might just be ready in time,' said Mum.

At midnight, when Dad got in from his shift, they still hadn't finished. Dad got stuck in immediately and they finally packed up at 1.27 a.m. The courgette and tomato sauce was ready and Mum had made enough plum puddings for all of her prospective diners.

'Everyone straight to bed now!' ordered Mum, ushering them all out of the kitchen. 'Tomorrow is going to be a big day and we'll need all the sleep we can get.'

*

'Wake up, you two!' said Mum, sticking her head round Eddie's door.

'Grim Grim Coyote,' murmured Fenda.

'Let me sleep!' hissed Eddie.

'It's the lunch day,' Mum reminded them.

At these words Eddie and Fenda's eyes sprang open and they leapt out of bed.

'Keep the noise down,' said Mum, 'Dad can still get another hour's sleep before he has to leave for his shift.'

Downstairs, the kitchen soon became a blur of activity. Trays were stacked, puddings were packed, the car was loaded up and in between all of this, Eddie and Fenda snatched a quick bowl of cereal for breakfast.

Mum drove the three of them to school and as she headed for the parking space beside the kitchen's back door, they all spotted a workman driving a small forklift truck, moving bricks towards the new block that was being built. Mum hurried into the kitchen, carrying a vast tureen of the tomato and courgette sauce, while Eddie and Fenda raced around school putting up the posters and menus they'd designed.

As soon as they finished, they went straight to the kitchen to give Mum a hand. There were plates to be stacked, cutlery to organize, lettuces to be chopped. When the bell went for the start of school, they ran into the playground and lined up with everyone else.

Eddie's teacher, Mr Armoury, was delighted to welcome Fenda, as were all of Eddie's classmates, some of whom had been involved in their own monster swaps. Fenda was thrilled to meet them all, but she and Eddie spent most of the next hour whispering about all of the things they'd have to do in the build-up to and during lunch.

Mr Armoury noticed how distracted they were but he let them be. He knew how important the lunch contract was to Eddie's mum. When break time arrived, Eddie and Fenda were first out of the classroom and they sprinted straight for the kitchen.

Mum was rushing about the place like a bluebottle who'd just downed a vat of fizzy drink. 'I'm so glad you're both here!' she called on seeing them. 'Can you bring in the foil from the car please?'

She chucked Eddie the car keys. He and Fenda hurried outside, Eddie unlocked the car and grabbed the rolls of tin foil. 'Why don't you grab the puddings,' he suggested to Fenda, pointing at the four trays of desserts.

'Got it,' nodded Fenda, lifting the pudding trays out. At that exact second they heard Mum yelling in the kitchen.

'Quick!' urged Eddie. He and Fenda put the foil and pudding trays on the ground and rushed inside.

A gigantic bee had entered the kitchen, but by the time they got there Mum had managed to steer it back out of a window.

'Thanks, guys!' She smiled goofily. 'Emergency over!'

They ran towards the door but as soon as they got outside again they stopped dead in their tracks.

'I think this might be a problem?' mouthed Fenda, as they both gaped at the forklift truck that had just reversed over the four dessert trays, leaving each one with a selection of completely crushed plum puddings.

'**N**ooooOO!' yelled Eddie as the forklift driver nodded at them and headed off, completely unaware of the damage he'd just caused.

'We can't let your mum see them,' said Fenda.

Eddie nodded, frantically trying to think on his feet. He ran in with the foil rolls, handed them to his mum and raced back outside to Fenda and the destroyed desserts.

'OK, let's get these inside,' he said, picking up two pudding trays while Fenda took the other two. They sidled back into the kitchen.

'OK?' asked Mum, looking up from the sink when they entered.

'Er ... yeah ... fine,' replied Eddie, quickly handing his two trays to Fenda and stepping between her and his mum's line of vision. 'What can we do next, Mum?'

'Could you two make the crosses in the potatoes please?' asked Mum, trying to look past Eddie. 'We'll stick them in the oven in about five minutes.'

'Sure,' called Eddie brightly, as Fenda dipped out of sight into the storage room. Not wanting to leave the puddings out and possibly seen by Eddie's mum, Fenda lifted the lid of a large white unit. It was very cold inside it and there was a loud buzzing noise coming from its innards. Fenda placed the trays inside the unit and turned the big white dial to **MAXIMUM**. That would be bound to stop the buzzing. She slammed the lid shut and raced back into the kitchen.

'Can you get the puddings out of the car?' shouted Mum, who was busy drying plates.

'All done,' replied Fenda, shooting Eddie a guilty look.

'Excellent!' nodded Mum appreciatively while checking her watch. 'Get cracking on those potatoes.'

Eddie had emptied the potatoes out of their sack on to a large work surface. He and Fenda took a knife each and began cutting an 'x' into the top and the bottom of each potato so that they'd cook through and be just the right fluffy texture.

'What are we going to do about the puddings?' hissed Fenda.

'I have no idea,' hissed back Eddie. *'We HAVE to think of something or else we'll completely ruin Mum's chances of winning that contract.'*

'Come on!' urged Mum. 'We need to get those potatoes in the oven very soon!'

Eddie and Fenda went into overdrive, cutting

'x's as fast as their hands and paws would allow them. Mum grabbed some steel baking trays and began spreading the potatoes out in neat lines.

'Faster!' she yelled.

They sped up again as Mum counted out the potatoes.

'Two hundred and forty-eight, two hundred and forty-nine, two hundred and fifty!' cried Mum triumphantly. 'Let's load them up!'

She pulled open the doors of the gigantic oven and shoved the trays inside. There were eight in all and they fitted in perfectly.

Mum turned the oven's large metal dial and pressed the ignition key to fire up the gas. The ignition started clicking but the whooshing noise of gas being released couldn't be detected.

'This often happens on my oven at home,' said Mum calmly.

She took her finger off the ignition, switched the gas dial off and waited a few seconds before trying again. Once more the ignition worked but the gas was not forthcoming.

'Here, let me have a go,' said Eddie.

He fiddled with the gas-connecting tube and tried again but there was no flow of gas.

'Leave it to me!' shouted Fenda. She pressed her nose against the ignition key and it broke off.

Mum, Eddie and Fenda looked at each other in complete panic.

'You've broken the oven,' said Mum in a strange, alien-like voice.

'Greetings, everyone!' declared a cool, business-like voice, as two people strode into the kitchen. 'I'm Mr Cheeves and this is Miss Briskit.'

'Greetings, Mr C and Miss B, I'm Fenda, a specially trained catering monster who is helping out with Mrs Wright's delicious, and might I say, highly nutritious sample meal,' blabbed Fenda. 'Allow me to introduce you to Mrs Wright herself – she'll just take you into the dining area and explain her long-term plans for if she wins the contract.'

Mum looked blank for a few seconds and then in a daze she walked towards the two inspectors and led them through to the dining area.

'What did you do that for?' demanded Eddie.

'We need time to think,' replied Fenda.

'No,' said Eddie, 'we need a MIRACLE! At this rate all the kids will be eating for lunch will be lettuce, with lettuce on the side, and lettuce pudding with a touch of tomato and courgette sauce!'

They stood staring at each other in horror but the silence was suddenly invaded by the distant sound of a wailing siren.

'That's probably my dad,' said Eddie.

'Your dad has turned into a lettuce?' asked Fenda.

'No, it's the siren of his fire engine. His crew cover this whole area. They're on their way to a fire.'

Two little sparks of hope suddenly sprang into Fenda's eyes. She flung open the oven doors and unravelled her arms at breakneck speed.

'Load me up!' she commanded.

'What do you mean?' demanded Eddie.

'Just give me the trays!' ordered Fenda.

181

With a confused shake of his head Eddie started loading the trays into Fenda's gigantically long arms. Within a minute she was holding all eight trays.

The siren was getting much louder.

'Open the door for me!' she said quickly.

Eddie ran over to the back door and pushed it open. Fenda hurried past him.

'Where are you going?' demanded Eddie, running after her.

'Just open that gate and let me out on to the road!'

Eddie pulled back the bolt on the gate and followed Fenda on to the pavement.

They could see Dad's fire engine pounding up the street towards them, its siren now a bellowing cacophony of noise.

'We'll be back as quickly as possible!' said Fenda. 'But your mum will have to stall them till then.'

'Back from where?' said Eddie in bewilderment.

Hang on to my legs!' shouted Fenda.

Eddie followed this command and a moment later, Fenda leapt into the air. Her springy feet catapulted her and her human friend high into the air.

Anyone who saw the fire engine pass by that morning would have been amazed to see, on the roof, a fluffy green monster with enormous arms, clutching eight baking trays of potatoes and an astonished-looking boy grasping on to her ankles for dear life.

Three minutes later the fire engine screeched to a stop outside an office block. There was a fire raging in a top-floor room, but the building had been evacuated and all the people working there were standing safely outside on the pavement.

Eddie's dad, three firemen and one firewoman jumped out and began setting up their ladders and unwinding their hose. Everyone in the street was so busy watching the fire crew that no one spotted the two figures leaping down off the roof of the fire engine and racing round the back of the building, where one of them raised her extraordinarily long arms towards the source of the fire.

*

Back in the school dining hall, Mum was talking about her incredible plans for what she would do if she won the contract, fully aware that she was buying time for her two kitchen assistants.

'My menus will be shown on a giant TV screen over there!' she was saying a bit too enthusiastically. 'And all my diners will have a swipe card so there'll be no actual money involved in paying for the lunches.'

She glanced over her shoulder for the tenth time hoping to see that somehow Eddie and Fenda had managed to get the oven lit, but there was no sound or sight from the kitchen.

'But what about *today's* sample lunch?' cut in Mr Cheeves. 'Surely you should be in the kitchen getting everything ready?'

'It's all completely taken care of,' replied Mum, trying to sound calm while her insides were dancing about like a bunch of hyperactive lizards. 'I'm a great believer in forward planning.'

But as the time hit half past eleven then quarter to twelve and finally five to twelve, both Mr Cheeves and Miss Briskit became extremely fidgety.

'We need to take up our positions now, Mrs

Wright,' said Mr Cheeves solemnly. He went to stand by the door joining the kitchen from the dining room, while Miss Briskit started roaming the room.

Mum nodded quickly and hurried into the kitchen.

A few seconds later the first sounds of running, chatter and laughter came from outside the door leading to the playground.

'They're here!' gasped Mum to herself.

And they were indeed; the first two classes were ready for lunch.

Mr Cheeves checked his watch.

'I'm very sorry, Mrs Wright,' he called over, 'but you're going to have to open that door pretty soon if you're to stand the slightest chance of winning this contract!'

With a heart as heavy as an ancient Egyptian sarcophagus, Mum slowly walked over to the doors, glanced over her shoulder one last time and then opened the door. Children came

flooding in and made straight for the serving hatch.

Mum made her way back to the kitchen on wobbly legs, only too aware of the fact that Mr Cheeves and Miss Briskit were about to watch children being offered the world's first *invisible* school lunch.

Mr Cheeves checked his watch again and tutted.

'Please begin serving NOW!' he commanded.

As Mum thought about hiding inside the broken oven, Eddie and Fenda barged into the kitchen, a melee of green arms and baking trays.

'Main course coming through!' called Fenda, rushing over to Mum with a huge collection of perfectly fluffy, exceptionally well-cooked baked potatoes.

Mum gazed at the two of them in shock.

'What are you waiting for?' shouted Eddie. 'Let's get serving!'

Ten seconds later the serving team were

in action. Fenda placed the potatoes on to the plates, Mum scooped the tomato and courgette sauce over them (which warmed up the minute it hit the baking hot potatoes), Eddie added some crisp salad and handed the plates out to diners.

Mr Cheeves stood by the serving hatch making notes on a clipboard while Miss Briskit roamed the dining hall asking children for their reactions to the potatoes.

'Nice!' said one.

'Fluffy!' said another.

'Not bad at all, but the sauce could have done with a tad more seasoning,' said Oliver Summersby.

Before the first classes had finished their potatoes, the second batch arrived and the hatch team carried on with their operation.

'OK,' said Mum a few minutes later, 'the first lot have finished their potatoes and are scraping their plates. I'm fine to carry on here; you two go and get the desserts.'

The desserts!

In all of the excitement of dealing with the potatoes Eddie and Fenda had completely forgotten about the ruined plum puddings.

'Yeah … OK … right …' mouthed a freaked-out Eddie.

'We're on it!' said Fenda, pulling her human friend towards the freezer room.

They crashed to a stop when they set eyes on the freezer. A huge foamy mound of ice had spread out of the freezer due to Fenda turning up the power dial to maximum.

'This can't be happening!' groaned Eddie.

But Fenda was already leaning over the freezer, scraping away some of the ice to locate the crushed plum puddings below. 'Get me a bowl!' she commanded.

Eddie ran out and came back with a bowl. Fenda scooped some of the plum filling from a pudding and placed it in a bowl with a swirl of ice. She took a quick lick.

'Freezy Plum Concoctions!' she announced.

Eddie put his finger into the mix and tasted it.

'Fenda, you are a GENIUS!' he cried.

'WHERE ARE THOSE PUDDINGS?' shouted Mum.

In a mad spin of activity, Eddie and Fenda started a remarkably speedy production line. When the first ten desserts were done, Eddie ran out with them.

'What are those?' hissed Mum, looking down at the desserts that Eddie had begun serving to the expectant diners.

'Slight menu change,' grinned Eddie sheepishly.

Mum looked at him as if he had just changed into a wombat vampire, but turned back to her potato seekers and left the desserts to Eddie.

Mr Cheeves continued writing furiously; Miss Briskit carried on with her questioning diners, this time about the plum concoctions.

'Fruity!' said one.

'Tangy!' said another.

'An extra gram of sugar might have removed the slight hint of sourness,' said Oliver Summersby.

Mum, Eddie and Fenda had never worked so hard, but groups of satisfied diners started leaving the canteen, praising the lunch they'd just had. As the time neared 1 p.m., the last children left the hall and the place was suddenly silent.

Mum shut the doors.

It was over!

The three lunchtime heroes gathered in the kitchen.

'How did you cook the potatoes?' whispered Mum.

'I just fired them up!' grinned Fenda. Eddie giggled.

'Right then,' said Mr Cheeves, as he and Miss Briskit entered the kitchen.

Mum, Eddie and Fenda stood to attention.

'Here are your marks,' said Mr Cheeves, 'starting with forward planning, for which we give you 9 out of 10.'

Mum, Eddie and Fenda beamed.

'The baked potato and sauce scored 8 out of 10,' added Miss Briskit.

'The salad scored 9 out of 10,' said Mr Cheeves.

Eddie tapped Fenda's shoulder. 'Amazing results!' he mouthed.

'And even though the dessert wasn't as advertised, we gave it 8 out of 10,' nodded Miss Briskit.

'For cleanliness of kitchen and all health and safety and serving requirements, you scored 9 out of 10,' finished Mr Cheeves, 'and I can let you know that this combined score of 43 out of 50 is the highest of any of the three potential contractors!'

'ULTRA FINE!' shouted Fenda, hugging both inspectors round their midriffs.

When they'd recovered from this ordeal, Mr Cheeves's tone suddenly turned stern.

'However,' he said, 'unfortunately your *time-keeping* let you down. You opened the dining hall doors three minutes late and because of this we *cannot* award the contract to you. We were very clear in our instruction DVD about how crucial time-keeping is to this entire operation. I'm sorry, but on this count you let yourselves down.'

Mum's hopeful smile turned to a look of despair.

But even as Mr Cheeves was relating this bad news, a very long green arm was twisting towards his wrist while several green fingers were getting to work.

Eddie felt as crushed as the plum puddings, but Fenda quickly piped up. 'Mr Cheeves sir, I think you'll find that your watch is actually three minutes *fast.*'

'I think not,' smiled Mr Cheeves. 'My time-keeping is perfect and just to prove it, listen to this.'

He quickly dialled a number on his mobile and put it on speaker phone.

'At the third stroke, the time will be one fifteen and forty seconds ...'

He looked down at his watch and his smile downturned into a frown.

'I ... I ... I ...' he spluttered.

He listened to check his watch was still ticking.

It was.

'Remarkable,' he murmured, 'that's the first time it's been out in thirty years.'

'These things do happen from time to time,' said Fenda casually.

'You were talking about time-keeping,' Eddie reminded him.

'Ah ... yes ... well, in light of this new discovery,' said Mr Cheeves, setting his watch back three minutes, 'Mrs Wright, it seems that you DID open the doors right on time and therefore ... I'm delighted to tell you that we will be awarding the twelve-month catering contract to you.'

'YES!' screamed Eddie, leaping up and swishing a fist through the air.

'ULTRA FINE!' yelled Fenda, springing up to the kitchen ceiling and coming back down just in time to exchange a high-five/ten with Eddie.

'That's amazing!' beamed Mum. 'Thank you so much! I'm delighted, I really am!'

'All of the paperwork will be sent to you,' said Miss Briskit. 'Congratulations, and well done on the plum concoction – it was delicious. I'd really like the recipe.'

Mum's face turned panic-stricken.

'We'll email it to you,' said Eddie quickly.

'That would be great,' smiled Miss Briskit, 'thank you.'

The inspectors nodded a brief farewell and then they were gone.

'OH YEAH!' screamed Fenda as she, Eddie and Mum linked hands and performed a wild celebratory dance. This was followed by a couple of minutes of hysterical laughter and when they finally calmed down, Fenda and Eddie told Mum everything – from the squashed plum puddings through cooking the potatoes in the flames of an office block fire, to the unintended discovery of the plum concoctions.

'Without you two I'd NEVER have done it!' grinned Mum. 'What a great team you are!'

Eddie and Fenda blushed modestly.

'Well,' said Mum, 'all we need to do now is clean this place thoroughly so it's ready for tomorrow. The new contract comes into force straight after the summer holidays, which is about ten weeks away. As the newly selected official caterer at Willow Street Primary, I need to start planning now!'

'How did it go?' asked a voice.

'*DAD?*' said Eddie.

'I had to know how the lunch went so we parked the engine outside,' explained Eddie's father, striding into the kitchen and looking at the three of them with an anxious, questioning expression.

'You'll never believe it,' said Mum. 'We got it!'

'NO?' exclaimed Dad.

'YES!' responded Eddie, Fenda and Mum.

'That's incredible!' cried Dad, hugging all three of them. 'Don't go away!'

He nipped outside and returned holding a large cardboard box with a picture on the side.

'And you see!' beamed Dad. 'I *did* spot the microwave was missing and I *did* figure out you wanted a new one!'

Mum stared at him in disbelief. 'But that looks like a normal one,' she pointed out. 'I thought you wanted to buy an ecologically-sound one ...'

'Eh?' said Dad. 'What are you talking ab—'

But before he could finish his sentence,

another figure burst through the doors.

'*Uncle Dan?*' cried Eddie.

Dan was big and burly and his cheeks were very red.

'I thought you were in Spain,' said Mum.

'I came back early,' replied Dan, 'and was just driving down the road when I saw the fire engine stop and spotted your dad coming in here. I have some very bad news.'

'Is it Auntie Sharon?' asked Eddie. 'Is she OK?'

'She's fine,' replied Dan, 'but someone broke into my allotment.'

Mum, Eddie and Fenda gulped simultaneously.

'They completely cleaned me out of tomatoes, courgettes and my prize lettuces!' seethed Dan.

Mum, Eddie and Fenda gulped again.

Eddie and Fenda edged back towards the door leading to the playground.

'I'll tell you what,' went on Dan. 'When I find

out who did it I'm going to kill them!'

'Er, Dan,' said Mum nervously, 'there's something I need to tell you.'

Dan looked at her and waited for what she had to say.

Eddie, however, wasn't prepared to wait.

He flung open the door to the playground, grabbed Fenda by her savoury tongue and shouted four crystal-clear words at his ashen-faced monster mate:

'RUN FOR YOUR LIFE!'